Dear Olivia,
Please don't be mad. It's sunny here. I'll be right back!
Guess what: Disneyland offered me a job as Snow
White, but they want me to dye my hair black!

Love, Mother

Shortly after Mother left I went a little crazy. I couldn't believe she was really gone. I dug in my heels against the passing days.

They slid by. Dirty dishes piled high. Salad greens composted in the fridge. Bouquets of chrysanthemums Mother had picked withered in every room.

I stayed up much too late every night, watching weird old movies on TV. Voices; I wanted to fill the house with sound. Dawn found me chilled and crumpled on the couch.

I ate a bunch of junk. My skin took on an unnatural sheen. My eyes looked like glazed doughnuts.

I didn't do my homework. I fell asleep in class.

Looking back, I know I thought: If I fall apart, Mother will come back and rescue me.

But she didn't come back, and I didn't fall apart. In the long run you have to save yourself. . . .

KUMQUAT MAY,
I'LL ALWAYS LOVE YOU

Other Bantam Starfire Titles you will enjoy:

Kumquat May, I'll Always Love You

Cynthia D. Grant

BANTAM BOOKS

TORONTO · NEW YORK · LONDON · SYDNEY · AUCKLAND

*This low-priced Bantam Book
has been completely reset in a typeface
designed for easy reading, and was printed
from new plates. It contains the complete
text of the original hard-cover edition.*
NOT ONE WORD HAS BEEN OMITTED.

RL 5, IL 12 and up

KUMQUAT MAY, I'LL ALWAYS LOVE YOU
*A Bantam Book / published by arrangement with
Macmillan Publishing Company*
PRINTING HISTORY
*Macmillan edition published April 1986
Bantam edition / April 1987*

*Starfire and the accompanying logo of a stylized star are
registered trademarks of Bantam Books, Inc. Registered in
U.S. Patent and Trademark Office and elsewhere.*

ISBN 0-553-26416-8

Published simultaneously in the United States and Canada

---

*Bantam Books are published by Bantam Books, Inc. Its trade-
mark, consisting of the words "Bantam Books" and the por-
trayal of a rooster, is registered in U.S. Patent and Trademark
Office and in other countries. Marca Registrada. Bantam
Books, Inc., 666 Fifth Avenue, New York, New York 10103.*

PRINTED IN THE UNITED STATES OF AMERICA

O   0 9 8 7 6 5 4 3 2

For Jack O'Hara,
Bigger than life

For Marjorie Jane Wusthof,
mother and child

For Pat Hare,
friend of the library, and friend

And for Dana Evans,
who named it

Eternity is not something that
begins after you are dead.
It is going on all the time.
We are in it now.

—CHARLOTTE
  PERKINS
  GILMAN

1

It is not widely known that my mother, Luna Lee Greene, has not been seen for two years today, this nineteenth of September.

"I'm just going out for a pound of margarine," she said, and disappeared.

The only person besides me in town who knows is my best friend, Rosella Jensen. As far as everyone else is concerned, Mother is still here.

It hasn't been easy. Fifteen-year-old girls aren't supposed to live alone, which I was, absolutely and abruptly. Grandmother had died the year before, and my father passed on to his reward when I was eleven. A promising lawyer and noted alcoholic, he died of acute procrastination at age thirty-four. So young, everyone murmured sadly, although they'd been expecting it for years.

I remember my father fondly and well through the warm fog of memories and Scotch he exuded with every breath. He could often be found at Iffy Murray's, as surely mounted on the polished bar stool as the ornamental wing on the hood of Grandmother's Hudson.

Our house is large and imposing; they used to call it the Mansion, but since my father never got around to lawn-mowing or maintenance, it resembled a beached showboat in a sea of ivy and hedges. This discouraged prospective clients. On clear days the air rang with the sound of his bouncing checks.

But back to Mother, lost on her mission of margarine . . . I can see her in the kitchen, putting on her old plaid coat. We were going to have spaghetti. She was going to come right back.

When she didn't, I wasn't too surprised; Mother was unpredictable. So I ate and went to bed. She still wasn't home the next morning, and that alarmed me, but we don't get many kidnappers in Kumquat, so I held my breath and hoped for the best.

Why didn't I call the police chief that day, or the next day, or the next? I was certain Mother would be home any second, and I didn't want to make a messy fuss.

The next thing I knew, it was two weeks later and I was holding a postcard from Disneyland.

Dear Olivia,
Please don't be mad. It's sunny here. I'll be right back!
Guess what: They offered me a job as Snow White, but
they want me to dye my hair black!

Love, Mother

Of course, the mailman noticed this. He said, "I didn't know your ma was out of town."

"She's not," I replied, thinking fast. "It's a joke; just an old friend of mine trying to be funny."

"I got a friend like that." The mailman smacked his

lips. "One Christmas he sent me some socks full of fish. A real practical joker."

"Sounds like a funny guy," I said, and then had to hear about every gift the friend had sent since 1954.

Living alone is not as hard as you'd imagine. In a way, I've always been on my own, as grown-up as my parents. I took care of us; did the laundry, fixed the dinner. When something big came up, I went to Grandmother. But as time went by, although she seldom complained, she had aches enough, and didn't need any extra. Besides, I didn't want her to know what a couple of *children* my parents really were. I tried to protect them, and I learned reticence early. It comes in handy now.

Only Rosella shares my deep, dark secret, and she wouldn't tell if she were tortured. I was determined that no one would discover Mother's absence, picturing the twilight world of foster homes, or worse, the *Twilight Zone* of Mother's brother, my Uncle Sargent.

He's older than Mother, by about two centuries. Like his parents, he believes that women are dim bulbs in a dark world. Not that he wants us brighter; he thinks men should lead the way, and if you argue, he says God said it first, and he's just delivering the message. Uncle Sargent always treated Mother as if she were a talking Pekinese. He and Aunt Cece are busily raising a litter of little lunatics.

I was not going to be shipped off to live with them, or to San Francisco and the grandparents I have never met. They probably wouldn't have taken me; they've never acknowledged I'm alive. They disowned Mother when she married my father. As if you could own your kid.

I would hold down the fort until Mother returned, making it appear that she was still here. How?

Every few months I have her skirts and sweaters cleaned. I renew her subscription to the *Kumquat Weekly Messenger.* At the market I buy the items that were always on her list: English muffins, mandarin oranges, coffee-colored pantyhose and Hershey kisses.

I purchase the books to which Mother was addicted. *Come into the world of Harlequin Romances . . .* Unfortunately, she seldom came out. In her reading room she devoured romance, each finished book a brick in the wall she built around her chair. The pharmacist's wife calls me every month when Mother's fresh shipment arrives.

When pressed, I even impersonate Mother on the phone. This is not something I enjoy. Most of the time my life makes sense, but I have to wonder when I pretend to be Mother; being me is confusing enough. And it makes me feel like a liar, which I hate, because I think of myself as so honest and straight, which is funny, because my whole life is a play.

It's been an odd two years. There have been many close calls. When people drop by to see Mother (they seldom do; she is fondly regarded as a dingdong), she is in the shower, heard gurgling in the background, while her lilac-scented soap perfumes the room. Or she's over in Cedar getting her hair done again, which frosts our local beauticians, Grace Nelson of Grace's Place, and Verda Mae at The Beauty Spot.

Or she's napping or shopping or otherwise indisposed . . . Time flies. People are busy with their lives. No one remembers when they last saw Mother. Folks don't come breaking down the door—although the PTA has tried to nab her, once even sending a contingent to surround the house. Mother later regretted (by phone) that she hadn't been home and, alas, was unable to attend the upcoming bake sale. However, she contributed ten dozen of her famous cocoa-cream clusters, which sold out in fifteen minutes and got her off the hook for some time.

I have learned a lot since Mother left.

I have learned to bake cocoa-cream clusters.

I keep the Plymouth running and the plumbing tight. The fireplace gets fed. The window screens are mended.

The house is huge and old and full of woodpecker holes; its tough skin of ivy keeps it standing. The inside is always reasonably clean, meaning dust is allowed to linger but not languish. I sleep downstairs in a bedroom off the kitchen. The second floor has been closed off; no sense heating those empty rooms.

Shortly after Mother left I went a little crazy. I couldn't believe she was really gone. I dug in my heels against the passing days.

They slid by. Dirty dishes piled high. Salad greens composted in the fridge. Bouquets of chrysanthemums Mother had picked withered in every room.

I stayed up much too late every night, watching weird old movies on TV. Voices; I wanted to fill the house with sound. Dawn found me chilled and crumpled on the couch.

I ate a bunch of junk; sugary stuff, frosted cereal with chocolate chips. My skin took on an unnatural sheen. My eyes looked like glazed doughnuts.

I didn't do my homework. I fell asleep in class. My teachers were aghast; they couldn't understand it and of course I couldn't explain.

Looking back, I know I thought: If I fall apart, Mother will come back and rescue me.

But she didn't come back, and I didn't fall apart. In the long run you have to save yourself.

Money has not been a problem, thanks to my grandmother, Olivia Shout Greene. Her husband took off when my father was a baby ("Weak men run in the family," she said), but she parlayed a small inheritance from her mother into a tidy fortune in corsets—which my father plundered (the fortune, that is) at every opportunity. Still, it kept us going through my father's perennial unemployment and after he died. He had no insurance. Grandmother paid off his debts.

The house is mine, free and clear. My tastes are simple, my needs are few: food, gasoline, property taxes, new jeans, an occasional tire. Grandmother's money will run out the month after I graduate from high school. I deliver the *Messenger* for movie money, although our local movie house usually features films you'd watch only if you were tied down. This week's double bill: *Fantasia* and *The Texas Chainsaw Massacre*.

I'm not sure what will happen after graduation in June. Rosella and I talked about going away to college; we sent for brochures and planned to room together. Her grades are excellent. She wants to be a doctor. My future is much less certain. I wanted to study psychology, so I could understand my family, but I can't leave Kumquat until Mother comes back or I might never find her again.

She didn't mean to leave me, I know that. She was on her way to Watson's Market. Then, outside in the plum-colored dusk, a light breeze driving dry leaves down the street, and Watson's so close to the Greyhound stop, a gleaming silver coach was probably parked at the curb, its engine throbbing with promise, its open door an invitation . . . It just happened. Life was always happening to Mother, washing over her, wave after wave. She loves me. She didn't leave me on purpose. She says she's coming home in every postcard.

They don't come often. Sometimes months go by without a word. Then, when I'm getting scared, when

I'm wondering if she's still alive, the Statue of Liberty appears in my mailbox, or it's Midnight at the Carlsbad Caverns, with a message in her delicate hand.

It's autumn again, and Mother's vivid in my mind, as the brilliant leaves whisper and fall to the ground, and the nights are startling with stars. The wind sings her name, Luna Lee, Luna Lee, and I can't help but hope that she will blow through the door, the mythical margarine clutched in her hands, her blue eyes dazzled by the bright kitchen light.

2

School was strange today. There was a rumor going around that Bunky Block got run down by a gravel truck, just outside the laundromat. Or that a gravel truck ran off the highway into the laundromat, where Bunky was kicking the Coke machine. Or that Bunky kicked some gravel at the laundromat window, and was spotted by owner Eugene Long, who tried to hit Bunky with a Coke bottle.

Much to everyone's disappointment, none of this happened. Bunky's case of athlete's foot had reached epic proportions and his mother kept him home.

Stories travel fast in Kumquat; about fifteen minutes from city limit to city limit. What's lost in accuracy is made up for in speed. Put your ear to the sidewalks and you hear them hum.

Like the gold that drew the first settlers, the kumquats are long gone. They couldn't take the winters; we get a little snow, just enough to send the kids running for rusty sleds and building slushy snowmen.

Kumquat's main industry is Kumquat. Big trucks roll up the highway, through the center of town, to the gravel pits, where huge hunks of Kumquat are carved out, loaded up and hauled away to build new towns. Someday all the earth beneath the highway will be gone, and Kumquat will be a bridge across the sky.

We do a little tourist business; the river draws rafters and fishermen who don't mind the wrecked cars half-buried in the banks to keep them from washing away. The sports shop sells duck stamps to big city hunters, and souvenir gold pans to the dreamers.

There's not much to do here. For thrills, the locals drive forty miles to Cedar to shop, or to Sacramento, three hours away. Or they cross the state line and head for the casinos skirting Lake Tahoe. This weekend Cora and Hank Smith won ten thousand dollars at the Midas Club, the first big win for anyone from town. Rosella and I joined the crowd outside the pharmacy after school to hear Cora tell the story.

"We're standing there at one of those big old dollar machines," Cora said. "Hank was dumping in dollars like there was no tomorrow, you know how he gets. And I tell him, 'Come on! The bus is leaving!' And he says, 'Hold on. This baby's going to pay off any second, I can feel it.'

"Well, that ticks me off because we always set a limit, then *he's* the one who wants to stay until he loses his shirt."

"So anyway," Dave said, trying to speed up Cora's story.

"So anyway, we're standing there and Hank's dumping in the dollars, and I say, 'Let's just break the damn bank!' And I take my last silver dollar and stick it in the machine next to his. . . . The next thing I know, some lady's screaming, 'You won! You won!' and the machine lights up, and bells are ringing—"

"How did you feel?" the pharmacist's wife asked, rapt. As usual, she was dressed in purple, a lavender chiffon shirtwaist.

"I felt. . ." Cora gave this some thought. "I felt like I did the time Hank rewired the house, and the current was running through the water pipes and I turned on the shower—BAM! It was just like that! People were going crazy and taking our pictures—"

"Did they give you the money in silver dollars?" Tommy Loors asked.

"Sure." Dave snickered and rubbed his bald head. "And a silver wheelbarrow to haul them."

"We had to fill out this form for taxes. Then we got a big check and two hundred silver dollars. You don't find that kind of change in the bottom of your purse everyday! But the thing that made me mad was, I looked so *bad*! I hadn't washed my hair, and I was wearing that old red dress—"

"I saw you in the paper," Dave said. "You looked like Orphan Annie."

"What will you do with all that money?" Eleanor Brown wondered.

"Get my hair done and buy a new dress!"

Everybody laughed.

"I know what they'll do with the money," Dave said. "They'll give it all back."

The crowd stopped laughing.

"Why would they do that?" demanded his good friend, Joe Pagnani.

"Yeah, why would we do that?" Cora was irate but wary.

"Because that's how it works! They'll invite you back up there, wine you and dine you. Bring the whole family! The club will pay! Rooms, drinks, meals, you name it. And while you're there, having such a fine time, maybe you'd like to gamble a little, just a little bit, then a little bit more . . . Wait and see. You'll get an invitation."

"We got one, for next month," Cora said sourly. "But that doesn't mean—"

Dave shook his head. "Those people don't let you go without a fight."

This observation called for a moment of silence. Then Verda Mae spoke up.

"If you don't give the money back, what will you do with it?"

We waited while Cora considered this. Trucks wheezed by on the highway.

"I think we'll move to Florida," she decided.

"Florida! What's in Florida?"

"Not much," said Rosella. "We were there."

"I don't know what's in Florida," Cora admitted, "but it sounds so pretty and warm, and I've always wanted to travel."

"You don't go to Florida to travel," Dave said. "You go there to die. You've got a few good years left."

"My, you're full of compliments today."

"It sure must've been weird, winning all that money." Tommy sighed.

"It sure was," agreed Cora. "I can't explain it."

The pharmacist came to the door in his spotless white uniform to make an announcement.

"You might like to know that the six-ounce bottle of Oil of Olay just went on sale."

"Whoooeee!" Dave said. "That's sure good news."

He spoke for us all.

Cora left for her beauty appointment and the crowd wandered away. Rosella went into the pharmacy to do some shopping for her mother. I sat outside on the Donated by the Kiwanis Club bench with Dave. His big pink hog, Jimmy Dean, stood curbside, contemplating the traffic.

Jimmy Dean comes down from the ranch in the back of Dave's pickup truck. When it's raining he rides in the cab. He's three hundred pounds of pig perfection; more loyal to his master than Lassie could ever be.

Jimmy Dean is the bane of Mayor Bobby Block's existence. The mayor had been glaring at him from the sidewalk in front of his hardware store. At last he couldn't stand it anymore. He bustled across the street. Dave started smiling.

"Dave!" the mayor bawled, inflating his chest. "How many times do I have to tell you to keep that hog in the truck?"

"Jimmy's not doing anything wrong," Dave said.

"We don't need a hog standing around the business district, maybe doing his business on the sidewalk."

"Jimmy always goes before we leave home." Dave was enjoying himself. He's known Mayor Bobby Block since the mayor was a little brat boy. Spoiled rotten, Dave said; always dressed up like Little Lord Fauntleroy. The other kids would grab him and roll him in the mud. Besides, Dave says, the name "Mayor Bobby" sounds like the host of some kiddy TV show.

The mayor was warming up. "Now, look here, Dave: we've kicked off our Beautify Downtown Kumquat campaign, and the first thing we've got to do is get rid of that hog!"

Joe Pagnani stepped out of Loretta's Bar & Deli. "Bobby, are you persecuting that poor little pig again?"

"Persecuting the pig!" The mayor's face was purple. "This thing is a public nuisance! Look at it! Big fat thing. It's obscene! It looks like somebody's behind walking around! Do you think tourists will stop and browse, or get something to eat at the Coffee Cup if they see that hog standing outside?"

"Jimmy's the Cough Up's best customer," Dave said. "He's crazy about Betty's cheese pockets. She baked him a batch the other day. But he won't touch her doughnuts. He's kind of a picky eater."

"You're supposed to eat hogs, that's what you're supposed to do!" squalled the mayor.

"You don't eat your pals." Joe shook his head sadly. "Some people have no appreciation for the finer things in life; like friendship, and loyalty, and balanced city budgets—"

"Don't change the subject!"

"What subject?" Dave said. "We're old men. We forget."

"Leave that hog at home where it belongs!"

"This is a free country," Joe said, "unless the City Council's passed some kind of ordinance."

"We're going to pass an ordinance about that hog! I'm warning you, Dave—"

"I wouldn't use that tone of voice if I were you," Dave advised. "Jimmy gets upset when you yell at me."

"I'll yell my head off if I want to!"

"Suit yourself." Dave shrugged. "But you'll have to take it up with Jimmy."

The mayor whirled around. Jimmy Dean stood behind him; his tiny ears flat, his fat face grim. A growl rumbled out of his throat.

"Get that thing away from me!"

"You heard the man, Jimmy."

Jimmy Dean advanced like a pink tank.

"Dave, call him off!"

"I'll try," Dave said. "But you know how pigheaded Jimmy can be."

"I'm warning you, Dave!" The mayor plunged into the street, nipping between a gravel truck and a giant Winnebago. The traffic drowned out whatever he was hollering. Jimmy went back to counting cars and Dave and Joe stepped into Loretta's.

The pharmacist's wife was ringing up Rosella's order and handing her a pink-striped bag.

"Liv, your mother's new books came in."

"Wonderful, she'll be so pleased."

The pharmacist's wife cracked open a box and dug out five fresh romances. The covers look identical, so they're numbered so you won't get confused.

She charged the order to Mother's account and tore off a strip of Blue Chip stamps. "How *is* Luna Lee? Seems like ages since I've seen her. I keep meaning to call but I've been so busy, with choir practice, and sorority projects . . ."

The pharmacist's wife is the Grand Matron of the local Psi Phi chapter. They do good deeds and wear formals and tiaras whenever they get the chance. Dave calls them the Sci-Fi Sisters.

".... time keeps rushing by. I mean, here it is September! In fact, we got in some Christmas cards; they're over there by the beach balls. Beautiful cards, little angels and everything. You might mention that to Luna Lee. And tell her I'll give her a call sometime. I've had my hands full with the pharmacy. And of course my back's been acting up. I sure wish we'd get another chiropractor in town, don't you?"

A while back we had a chiropractor, a Dr. Richard "Dick" Richards. He breezed into town in a red Cadillac and rented the suite over the pharmacy. He hung out his shingle and went into business; worked the whole town over pretty good. The bank president swore by him. He treated the high school athletes. The pharmacist's wife saw him twice a week; she claimed his hands worked wonders.

It turned out he wasn't a chiropractor at all; just a real estate salesman down on his luck. The *Messenger* went to town with banner headlines, ringing rhetoric, and dozens of indignant letters to the editor. Everyone regretted that they'd taken off their clothes for a land broker from New York.

"... might not have been a real doctor but at least he took me seriously. Dr. Johnson acts like I'm imagining the pain. The pain is not in my head, it's in my back! It's an old ballroom dancing injury."

I said yes and mm-hmm. One thing I've learned is this: People are mostly interested in themselves. But they also love good listeners like me.

I don't care to talk about myself; there's too much I don't want to tell. I've lived in Kumquat all my life and the only person who really knows me is Rosella.

"—of course, Merry's a lot like me. I was a dreamer,

too. But the time comes to put away dreams and grow up.''

"Yes, ma'am," I agreed.

Merry (Meredith Ann) is her daughter, and one of my dearest friends. She's a strawberry blonde with a peach-colored face and freckles that flare when she blushes. She says whatever pops into her head, which is why I haven't told her my secret.

"Will that be everything, Liv?"

"Yes, thanks."

Rosella decided to buy a bottle of Oil of Olay.

"A wise purchase, Rosella. That's a very good price."

We made it outside before we burst out laughing.

"A ballroom dancing injury!" Rosella gasped.

We stopped to gas up the Plymouth. I went inside to pay Ginny. She was expertly polishing the blood-red fingernails that are the reason the station is self-service. Her big dream in life is to do hand commercials for moisturizers and dish soaps that soften as you clean. She's treasured those fingernails since childhood, and her brother has the scars to prove it.

Cruising north on the highway, smiling and silent, we absorbed the afternoon. The light was as pure as Crystal Creek, and bright leaves fell like confetti.

It's so simple with Rosella. My fences come down. She knows me inside out. She moved to town shortly before Mother flew the coop, but I feel as though I've known her forever.

We listened to the radio. The reception's not too good; there are too many mountains between here and Sacramento. What comes out often sounds like the Muzak in hell, but once in a while the conditions are right, and that crazy disc jockey stops screaming and plays some song we really like, and we feel so . . . big and happy in the movie about our lives, fast friends rolling down the highway, easy as the endless breeze.

We hit the tail end of a Stones' song. Rosella thinks they're awful. *Oooooh, baby, you're lazy, you're crazy. Honey, I hate you. Kiss me* . . . That's Rosella's impersonation of the Stones.

"Baby, I *love* you! The Stones!" screamed the deejay. "Say, speaking of love, and who isn't these days…Guys: Are the gals stepping out on you, even on airplanes? If you were the last man on earth, would the last gal tell you, 'Hey, let's just be friends?' Maybe it's your hair! Let The Style Station take care of your hair care needs! They'll give you the kind of hair that makes people stop and say: 'He knows where it's at, and it's at The Style Station.' That's The Style Station, 1621 Auburn Boulevard, where they care about your hair care problems."

Rosella laughed and leaned out the window. The wind made her dark hair dance.

We turned off the highway at Red Mountain Road and drove out to Man Eater Lake. It's an old quarry, fed by springs and veined with tunnels and caves. Beneath its smooth face, currents move swiftly. Whirlpools flower and fade. Old-timers claim it's bottomless and try to scare away kids with the story of the Honeymooning Couple, whose canoe capsized and disappeared. Her flower-trimmed hat was found floating on the water. The bodies were never recovered.

There are signs posted: No Boating. No Wading. Anyone with sense leaves the lake alone. But it's pretty to look at and a popular spot with picnickers and lovers.

I parked the car and we took the path leading down to the shore. Rosella carried cups of coffee from the Cough Up, and I brought the doughnuts, still warm in their bag.

We settled where we always sit, a polished silver log at our backs, the glittering lake at our feet. The sun was strong as summer and the breeze was laced with pine.

Rosella described the dress she's designing in Home Ec. She sews like a dressmaker to the queen; clean-lined and elegant as the poetry she writes. Any talents I have remain hidden. Sometimes I think I use up all my imagination convincing the town that Mother is still here.

Rosella has lived other places besides Kumquat and she says people here are nuts. Nice, but nuts. I can't compare, since I haven't been anywhere, but I expect she knows what she's talking about. She almost always does.

She's the person I would have chosen for my sister. She kept me from exploding when Mother disappeared. We never run out of things to talk about. We know each other's minds.

So much in the world defies description. Like the way you feel at night, sitting on the front porch, dazzled by the darkness and the stars, millions of stars, trillions of stars, spilling on forever, no city limits, no dead ends, no fences. An end to fences. Infinity.

And hummingbirds. And skin up close. And hair and clocks and weather and brains. (Brains! How in the world do they work? How can they hold all those memories and faces?) And fire, and fruit trees, and music, and babies, growing in their mothers' bellies. . . .

I have no words to express my amazement.

Fortunately, I need no words with Rosella. "Sure is a gorgeous day," she agreed.

I closed my eyes and sailed away. Rosella rapped my knee.

"Look at that." She pointed to a whirlpool, waves swirling in giddy circles.

"Did we eat all the doughnuts?" I rooted through the bag.

"Forget the doughnuts. Look!"

A man was rising from the whirlpool—a man! Head and neck and golden shoulders; water streaming down his naked chest, cutoffs clinging to his narrow hips. Flinging back his long black hair, he looked directly at me; his green eyes showing no surprise, as if he had always been walking out of the lake, and I had always been watching him.

"Olivia," he said, and my tongue unlocked.

"Lord!" I gasped. "It's Raymond Mooney!"

3

Raymond was a boy when he left Kumquat, and this sleek, wet creature was a man. In his eyes I saw that I had changed, too. We moved toward each other. He held out his hand.

"What in the world are you doing in the lake?" I asked idiotically. What was he doing in Kumquat? The last I'd heard, he and his family were way down south, near Los Angeles.

"Swimming." He grinned and skinned back his hair. "Are you surprised to see me?"

"Surprised! You sure—" I was babbling. "You can't swim in there. It's dangerous! Didn't you see the signs?"

"Thank heaven you got here in time!" Raymond clutched at his heart. Then he seemed to spot Rosella. His smile tightened and his eyes narrowed. I'd seen that look before, when Grandmother stepped out the door with chunks of cake or watermelon wedges. Raymond's green eyes focused, accurate as radar, his hand homing in on the biggest piece no matter how much she juggled the plate.

He measured and weighed Rosella. "Who's that?"

"My best friend, Rosella."

"She's black."

"You're kidding!"

Raymond didn't smile. "Didn't use to be blacks in town."

"Things change," I said, suspecting that Raymond had changed more than I knew. Of course Rosella was black. I'd noticed it when we met, just as she'd noticed I was white. Our difference is skin deep and unimportant, but it makes a difference to some people in town, who mask it with extra politeness that Rosella sees right through. In their eyes, she's an outsider, but I'm an outsider, too.

"Come on," I told Raymond. "I want to introduce you."

Rosella stood and brushed off her pants. Her face was

smooth, but her eyes were wide with the spectacle of Raymond's entrance.

"Rosella Jensen, this is Raymond Mooney. We used to be little kids together."

"Hi," Rosella said. Raymond nodded.

"He moved away before you came to town."

"I remember you mentioning him," she said.

He smiled. "We sure had some good times together. It was a long time ago, wasn't it, Livvy."

"You look so different!" I blurted.

"You too. I like your hair long. You used to have those little things sticking out from the sides of your head."

"My ears, you mean." He was making me blush. "I'm the same, just taller."

"Nope, you've changed. You're all grown up."

I felt huge and confused. I seldom think about my body; it's the clothes my brain wears to town. Like the Plymouth, it could use some work, but it gets me around.

We were staring at each other. I had to say something.

"I can't believe you're really here."

"It's true." He stroked his chest. "In the flesh. We've got so much to talk about, Livvy."

"You're cold."

"What?"

"Goosebumps," I said. They rippled across his bare skin.

"Guess I'll put on my shirt." He retrieved it from the bushes. "Liv, can you give me a ride back to town?"

It was strange, walking beside him up the path. There wasn't room for the three of us. Rosella walked ahead.

"It's funny, running into you here. I was going to

come by your house," Raymond said. "Ma would like you to come for dinner."

"I can't. We always study together."

"We?"

"Rosella and I."

"You can study anytime. Isn't that right, Rosella?"

"Pardon?"

"See? It's all settled." He grinned.

He slid into the front seat. Rosella rode in back.

"So what are you doing in Kumquat?" I asked. "Visiting?"

Raymond grimaced. "It's a long story. I'll tell you later."

After Rosella was gone, he meant.

I dropped her off in front of her house. Her mother waved from the window.

"You sure you don't mind if we don't study tonight?"

"Of course not," Rosella said. "Nice to meet you, Raymond."

"Sure," he said. "See you again sometime."

I stopped by my house to check the mail. There was nothing but a flyer from J.C. Penney's.

"Shouldn't you tell your mother you'll be gone?"

"Mother isn't home right now," I said.

I headed the Plymouth toward Raymond's old house, then remembered he hadn't lived there for five years.

"By the way, where are we going?"

"Railroad Ave. We're renting Old Man Ridley's place. For now. We'll buy a house later. Maybe one of those new ones up on the hill."

"Those are expensive."

"Things are different now, Liv. My dad had a really great job in L.A. He made a lot of dough."

"What happened? Did he get fired or something? I'm sorry, it's none of my business—"

"Stop the car."

"Right here?"

"Right here." His face was grim. "We have to talk."

I pulled the Plymouth to the side of the road. Raymond switched off the ignition.

"I'm going to tell you something, Liv, but you have to promise—promise!—that you'll never tell. Never. It's a matter of life or death."

"Raymond—"

"I'm serious! Do you promise?"

"I promise! You know I'm not a blabberhead."

"I know." He sighed, gazing at the main drag. "This town is such a pit . . . It's just that I have to be so careful. My father—" He leaned toward me, lowering his voice. "My father—you'll think I'm crazy but it's true . . . My father—"

"Just tell me!"

"Okay, but you won't believe me."

"I'll believe you!"

"My father's with the CIA," Raymond said.

"You're kidding."

This news was a tremendous shock. Mr. Mooney was the last person on earth I could picture as a secret agent. No one would suspect him. He's a short, silent, colorless man, who looks like he's gone through the wash too many times. Having that batch of Mooney kids seemed to use up all his juice. He had held lots of jobs around town, but not for long, and none that would have prepared him for his current assignment.

"I don't understand. Why is the CIA in Kumquat? Nothing's happening here."

"Exactly," Raymond said.

"Exactly what? It doesn't make sense."

He shook his head. "I've said too much already. No

one is supposed to know. And whatever you do, don't mention it to my folks. They'll kill me if they find out I told you.''

"I wish I knew what you were talking about.''

"You will,'' Raymond promised. "Very soon.''

As we drove I wondered if the day would ever come when he would know my secret, too.

In days gone by, suppertime at the Mooneys' was like a Ma and Pa Kettle movie; the chaos was so colossal that you couldn't believe that anything would end up on the table.

Things hadn't changed much. There were just as many kids, only bigger, and louder; a half dozen of them, ranging in age from eight-year-old Rory to eighteen-year-old Raymond, with Daryl, Dwayne, Sammy and Sophronia in between. I couldn't keep the boys' names straight, but neither could their mother.

"Daryl, I mean Sammy, go wash your hands. Where's Rory?''

"Right here, Ma.''

"Not you, I mean Dwayne.''

Old Man Ridley's place was small, and it was busting at the seams with the Mooneys' stuff: toys, shoes, clothing, unpacked boxes and scabby furniture. A big color TV stayed on throughout the meal so Sophronia could watch her favorite show. Every show is Sophronia's favorite.

"Well, Livvy!'' Mrs. Mooney roared when we were jammed around the table, swiftly swapping plates of tomatoes, hamburgers and bread. "You've sure grown up pretty, just like your mother. She was always so nice and skinny, unlike yours truly.'' Mrs. Mooney laughed, her underarms jiggling. "How *is* Luna Lee these days?''

"Just fine, Mrs. Mooney.''

"Tell her to come by and see me sometime."

"I will. She's kind of busy."

"Aren't we all." Mrs. Mooney sighed and shook her head. "I swear, the time goes flying by. Your children are babies, then the next minute—*ask,* Rory; don't grab. Chew with your mouth closed, Dwayne. More burgers, Big Ray?"

Mr. Mooney silently accepted and consumed the food. He looked worn down as a pencil stub, bestirring himself only to lean across the table and give smart-mouthing Sammy a rap to the crewcut.

". . . I mean, look at Raymond! He's taller than me!" swooned Mrs. Mooney. "I'll bet you didn't even recognize him, Liv. Of course, I'd know you anywhere; you look so much like Luna Lee. She and your daddy made such a handsome couple. You look some like him, too."

"What color were his eyes?"

"His what? Daryl, take your elbows off your plate."

"Do you happen to remember the color of his eyes?"

Mrs. Mooney frowned, recollecting. "Well, they were black, weren't they? Black, I think."

"Brown," said Mr. Mooney.

"You sure, Big Ray?"

"Brown," he repeated. That was all he said all night.

"Maybe so. It was so long ago," mused Mrs. Mooney. "He was such a young man when he died."

A commercial came on and I spoke to Sophronia. She reluctantly turned her gaze from the dancing deodorant cans.

"What did you say?"

"You'll have to excuse my sister. She's addicted," Raymond said.

"Shut it, dipstick."

"That's not nice," her mother said.

"Excuzay *mwa*." Sophronia rolled her eyes. She

looks like she weighs about ninety-eight pounds, but eats like a snake, her jaws unhinging to encompass each heaping forkful. I'd never seen skin so skim milk pale, as if only colorless food passes her lips; marshmallows, boiled Wonder Bread.

"I was wondering if you're glad to be back in Kumquat."

"You've got to be kidding! I wouldn't come here to die!"

"Sophronia," her mother said.

"Besides, the reception has been lousy," she continued.

"You mean people haven't been friendly?" I inquired.

"The *TV reception!*" She regarded me as though I were a moron.

"Tell Olivia your theory, honey," prompted Mrs. Mooney.

"It's in the air," Sophronia said, staring at the tube.

"I beg your pardon?"

"It's in the air! All the TV shows, every minute of the day and night. And we're just like antennas, picking up all those signals—"

"That is the biggest crock," Raymond said.

"You don't know anything about it! If it's not true, then how come the words from some old *I Love Lucy* just pop into my head?"

"Because you're nuts."

"It's a scientific fact!"

"Sure is."

"Don't you two get started," said Mrs. Mooney. "Sophronia's very interested in television, Liv. She plans to be a soap opera actress."

"Watching TV doesn't make you an actress," snorted Raymond. "You have to have talent."

"Like you, I'm sure," Sophronia snapped.

"You said it, I didn't."

"Why don't you soak your big fat head, if you can fit it into the toilet?"

"Not at the table," warned Mrs. Mooney. "Who would like some chocolate pie?"

Everyone wanted chocolate pie. Mrs. Mooney isn't the world's greatest cook, but anything I don't have to make tastes good to me.

Sammy and Dwayne got stuck with the dishes while Sophronia studied a screaming comedy. Raymond invited me into his room to talk. He shares the room with Daryl and Rory, who occupy a rickety bunk bed in one corner. Raymond's single bed was a tight white island in a sea of tattered comic books and socks.

I sat on a wooden chair by the nightstand. Raymond left the door open so his mother wouldn't have a fit.

"Want to hear the radio?"

"Sure."

He tuned in the Eternal Deejay. Day or night, the deejays at that station sound like the same guy.

"You like music, Liv?"

"Yes."

"What kinds of music?"

"All kinds, I guess."

"Me too. Will you go to the Halloween dance with me?"

I laughed. He hadn't even started school, and here he was booking me for a date a month away. It was funny to think of me and Raymond on a date. Years ago, I never could have pictured it.

"What's funny?" His eyes were angry. He thought I was laughing at him.

"Nothing. I was just thinking how grown-up we are."

His smile made the shabby room bloom.

We talked . . . There was so much catching up to do. I

brought him up to date on developments in town. He told me what his family had been doing. When they moved to Los Angeles, his dad made pots of money. They bought a big fancy house; it sounded fabulous. There was a huge black-tiled pool made to look like a lagoon. And a sauna, and a four-car garage. Everyone had their own bedroom, and there were leather recliners and corduroy-covered couches and real Persian rugs and a state-of-the-art stereo system . . . Everything but the new color TV was in storage now, while Mr. Mooney was—Raymond's whisper tickled my ear—undercover.

"Undercover!"

"Keep your voice down!"

"How could your father be a spy? You said . . ."

Daryl came in and Raymond shot me a look. Then he told me about Los Angeles. It was throbbing with fantastic people and places. There were beaches and clubs and symphonies and museums and a community theater where Raymond starred in plays. He was the kid, Nick, in *A Thousand Clowns,* and he showed me the program with his name on the cover and a glowing review from the *L.A. Times.*

> *Talent scouts would do well to catch* A Thousand Clowns *at the Belson Community Playhouse. Newcomer Raymond Mooney, Jr., makes the role of "Nick" his own. This young man has the flame of talent crackling all around him.*

The flame of talent.

I said, "It sure must've been hard to come back to Kumquat."

"You ain't kiddin'. But like the saying goes: 'A diamond is a lump of coal that stuck with it.' I'm sticking with it."

He told me that he had decided to make acting his career, and that the famous Pasadena Playhouse had offered him a scholarship, and that UCLA had approached him, too.

Suddenly, I envisioned Raymond on TV, and on the big screen, in the movies; his handsome face magnified, his eyes star-sized. I heard myself saying, I knew him when . . .

Mrs. Mooney stood in the doorway, smiling. "Son, it's time to walk Olivia home."

"I've got my car."

Raymond offered to accompany me. I insisted I'd be fine all the way out to the Plymouth. Raymond drove.

The fat, buttery moon filled the sky, spilling inside me. I was too happy to talk. There are so many kinds of silence.

We parked beside my dark house. "Looks like your mom went to bed," he said.

"Well, goodnight."

"Goodnight." He handed me the keys. "It sure is good to see you, Livvy. I thought of you so often, and I meant to write."

"Me too. I'm not much of a letter writer."

"Anyway . . . I'm back now." He raised one finger and gently traced my cheek. "It feels so good to be with you, Liv. Life has been too strange lately, and you're so nice and normal."

"That's me."

"We'll be just as close as we used to be. No secrets between us. I promise."

My skin was alive where he'd touched me. No one, adult or child, had touched me for months. I sail through life like a solitary boat.

"Goodnight, Raymond." I got out of the car and

started across the lawn. At the door I stopped and called his name.

"Raymond?"

In the moonlight his face shone white as ivory, burning with eyes so fiercely warm I ached to tell them the truth. No secrets between us. Raymond, you won't believe this, but Mother—

"What is it, Liv?"

"I'm glad you're back."

I unlocked and entered my empty house.

4

Although I live alone, my family surrounds me. They inhabit every room of this house. They fill the closets with their clothing. They cover the walls with their photographs and books.

I feel them all around me, and in me. Their voices echo in the words I say.

Grandmother taught me how to say no. I stood beside her as she arranged my father's funeral. Cloistered at home, Mother had vetoed a cremation; she wanted him to lie down and take a long rest. Grandmother disapproved, but she chose a handsome coffin. The undertaker was intent on keeping it open during the funeral. Grandmother stressed that this was not what Mother preferred.

"I understand completely," the undertaker gushed. That gush was fatal. "But if you'll permit me to say so, we like to show off our work."

Grandmother's jeweled hand slammed his desk. "I don't give a good damn *what* you like! You'll keep that coffin closed!"

And he did.

Grandmother didn't want, and didn't have, a coffin; just a shockingly small cardboard box. People don't amount to much; a handful of ashes and bits of bone. I scattered her out back, at the base of the soaring redwood tree she'd planted as a new bride. Mother wept and watched from the kitchen window.

I was frightened and sad, and I knew that I would miss her, but Grandmother had had it with living. She was ill and in pain, and very old. We never knew how old; she kept that to herself. Once, Mayor Bobby came right out and asked her age! "Can you keep a secret, Bobby?" she asked, leaning out the window of her green Hudson. "Yes, ma'am, I surely can." "Good!" Grandmother snapped, hitting the gas. "So can I!"

A beautiful woman with fine, strong bones, she did not enjoy seeing the bloom decay. One morning she announced that her pores were so large they were apt to run together into one big hole that would swallow her face. This statement was unlike her, one of her bone-aching days. She was a resolute woman who looked directly at life, without glasses, without flinching, for eighty-odd—some mighty odd—years.

Losing my father hit her harder than she ever admitted. It's unnatural for a mother to bury her child. But this was typical of my father, never an average kid. He would have loved his funeral, which was doomed from beginning to end.

Since my father was not a believer, the funeral was held in the Kumquat Grange Hall. Guest organist Edith Lynch brought her electric Hammond from home.

The folding chairs filled up nicely. Half the town came out of respect for Grandmother; the other half came because my father owed them money, and they wanted to make sure this wasn't another of his stunts. I sat up front, between Grandmother and Mother; Mother in the pale yellow tea dress she wore to her wedding; Grandmother in black and scowling, sorrowful and angry.

The mayor and his wife stepped in. Mrs. Block started to sit, then got talking to my Uncle Sargent and Aunt Cece, who had flown in on their brooms for the occasion. Uncle Sargent and Mrs. Block went to school together. They shot indignant looks at the casket.

Meanwhile, the mayor, to be polite to the pharmacist's wife (some say he's overly attentive), reached back and got her a folding chair—the very chair his wife had intended for her own, and toward which, at that moment, her bottom was aimed.

She hit the floor with a shriek and a thud. Mother burst out laughing. I was glad for that laugh, knowing how badly Mother needed it, how gravely she was wounded, but some folks found it alarming. Uncle Sargent glared at her until she closed her pink-rimmed

eyes in shame, prompting Grandmother to turn her
scowl on him until he looked away.

Dave, slick and stiff in his suit, never recovered from
Mrs. Block's abrupt decline. His stifled laughter continued to erupt until he gave up and left the room.

Reverend Boles from the Methodist Church did the
service. He said lots of nice things about my father and
not one person snickered. Then we all left the Grange
Hall and drove to the cemetery. It was a bright spring
day and the wind was coltish.

Holy Cross Cemetery is high on a hill overlooking
the river and the highway. The wind and the gravel
trucks drowned out all but the highlights of the Reverend's speech: *peace . . . love . . . life everlasting . . .* Then
my father went into the ground. Mother was stunned
and couldn't seem to comprehend what was happening.

Then friends came by our house for coffee and cake
and to tell funny stories about my father. Uncle Sargent
and Aunt Cece came, too. In fact, they had arrived so
soon after he died that I suspected they'd been parked
around the corner, waiting, for years.

They consoled Mother for only five minutes before
she collapsed and had to be carried to her room. Uncle
Sargent fixed me with his hard blue eyes and said:
"Your father is singing with the angels now."

"Then who was in that box?"

Uncle Sargent said it was difficult to explain and
wouldn't discuss it further.

Since mentioning my father made Grandmother sad
and angry, and made Mother's eyes look like cornered
canaries, I seldom brought up the subject of my father
in the ground at Holy Cross Cemetery. It was always as
if he had just stepped out to Iffy Murray's and was
always, and never, on the verge of coming back.

Like Mother. I wish she'd send me a postcard. The

last I heard, she was guiding trail rides at Sky Ranch in Montana. The Mother I knew was afraid of horses. The Mother I knew has become someone else.

When my father died, I truly missed him, but I had missed him all my life. Even when he was in, he was frequently out—like a light, snoring on the sofa. Most of the time he was somewhere else; downtown, cracking his dice cup on the bar, rolling the other regulars for drinks.

There are three bars in Kumquat. Loretta's serves food and is a family-style place. Danny's Inferno is down the block. Danny's is where you go when you want a chair broken over your head. Once a month the mayor drives over there from his hardware store, pries the plywood off the windows and installs fresh glass.

Then there's Iffy Murray's.

Iffy Murray's was my father's bar.

I know if I passed through that door today the room would be unchanged; identical to all the times I saw it with my father. Sometimes he'd take me for walks around the block. We'd always end up on those slippery stools.

Iffy's bar was okay; no broken glass. Iffy's a big guy and he squashes fights fast. At one time he wrestled under the name Elegant Earl. There are framed photos of him as a young man in tights; also a photo of his boxer dog, Walt.

Vases of dusty artificial flowers decorate the six round tables. High stools with patched vinyl seats hedge the long, slick bar. The mirror behind Iffy is twenty feet across. A hairline crack at the left-hand side has been lengthening year by year at a glacial pace. My father always sat in front of the cash register so he wouldn't have to face his reflection.

Iffy was nice to me. He gave me unsalted peanuts (he has blood pressure problems), and he let me play the jukebox for free. All the songs were at least ten years old; mostly country westerns and the polkas Iffy prefers.

He let me examine his collection of watches, pinned by their straps to the wall behind the bar. People gave them to Iffy to keep until they could pay their bar bills. There were all kinds of watches; some cheap, some gold, some with Roman numerals that glowed in the cave of my cupped hands. Iffy knew I would be gentle with them. When my father died, Iffy gave me back his watch.

It's hard to know where my father leaves off and the memory of him begins. I know he was handsome and he laughed a lot. He slept in the afternoon and sometimes he cried. Looking back, little else seems certain.

When I close my eyes and quiet my mind, I can hear my father singing, the song as clear as when I lay in bed and heard him waltzing home down the dark street.

Kumquat may, I'll always love you,
Kumquat may, I'll always care,
Kumquat may, we'll be together,
Someday, somewhere

Kumquat may, I won't regret you,
Kumquat may, I will be true,
Kumquat may, I won't forget you,
How could I forget a love like you?

At first I thought he was singing about May Logan, who worked part-time in Iffy Murray's bar. This seemed unlikely, even to a child like myself, because nobody in Kumquat is more truly married than May and her husband, Jack. Childhood sweethearts, they're madly in love after three kids and thirty years. Some folks think that's strange, them being so close that separating the two would produce the sound of a plumber's helper leaving a kitchen sink. Personally, I think it's lucky and lovely that they found each other in this world.

No, my father laughed, he wasn't singing about May Logan. It was a play on words: Come what may, Kumquat may—*don't you get it, Livvy?*

I got it, and it's never left me. It's the song I hear when I shut my eyes and see my father waltzing with Mother. It's the song my father sings with the angels as his dice cup cracks like thunder. It's the song organist Edith Lynch would have played at my father's funeral, if I were God and had the magic that moves musician's hands.

5

"You're not going to tell him, are you?"

I knew exactly what Rosella meant. She meant: Don't tell Raymond about your mother. She doesn't trust him. They rub each other raw.

"No, I haven't told him. Yet."

"You're going to?"

"I don't know. Maybe."

It was lunchtime at Kumquat Unified School. Rosella and I sat on the lawn eating our sandwiches, beneath a liquid amber tree raining wine-colored leaves.

"Aren't you afraid he'll blab it around?"

"Raymond never had a big mouth."

"Maybe he's changed." Rosella bit into her apple, her teeth splitting the fruit with the clean crack of a wedge in wood.

"He's asked me to go to the Halloween dance."

"Are you going?"

"I might. What about you?"

She shrugged. "I haven't decided yet."

"Me neither." This wasn't true. Of course I would go to the dance with Raymond. Rosella knew it too.

"Do whatever you want," she said. "But if people find out you're living alone—"

"They won't," I assured her.

"I hope not, for your sake."

Was she worried for me, or for herself; worried that Raymond could take her place? No. Rosella would never stoop to jealousy. My face burned with shame.

Merry rushed over to us, gasping. With Merry, rushing and gasping are the usual course of events. Consequently, she's slightly lightheaded, but a real nice kid.

"That Raymond Mooney! He's something!" she blurted. "I can't believe it! He used to be such a little twerp! And now he's such a—"

"—big twerp," Rosella said.

"No! He's—gosh! He's so handsome!" Merry burbled. "Did you know he has a black belt in karate? It's true! He just flipped Bunky Block right over on his back! His body's practically a deadly weapon!'' Merry fluffed her hair like she was tossing a salad. Her freckles flushed pink. "And guess what else!"

"What else?" Rosella obliged.

"He's going to be an actor! He even met Donald Douglas!"

"Donald Douglas?" I was in the dark.

"The TV star! He's going to go to Pasadena Playhouse, where all those famous stars got started. They've already accepted his application! He's staying at Old Man Ridley's house."

"Donald Douglas is staying at Old Man Ridley's? My, he's sure come down in the world."

"Rosella, you know I'm talking about Raymond! They're staying there until they build a new house. Mr. Mooney's getting a great big settlement, because he got injured on his last job. That's why he gimps around," Merry confided.

The hardest part about knowing a secret is resisting the urge to tell; resisting the thrill of those shocked faces: *You're kidding! Mr. Mooney's in the CIA?*

I kept my promise to Raymond—at a cost: I had never kept a secret from Rosella before.

Merry twirled on her toes. "I'm so glad he came back to Kumquat!"

"Oh, me too," Rosella murmured.

The bell rang. Kids of all sizes flew by. Rosella and I headed for our English class. As I slid into my seat, Raymond smiled across the aisle at me. He looked grown up enough to be the teacher.

Miss Maxwell gave us a short written assignment: describe the most fascinating person we'd ever met. Fifteen minutes later she called for volunteers. Sue

Cooper's hand is always flapping in the breeze, so Miss Maxwell chose Raymond. He stood and read this:

"In all modesty, I am the most fascinating person I have ever met. Forever changing and evolving, I remain a mystery, a stranger, even to myself. What man can truly say he has explored the depths of his character, or can accurately predict his reaction to every situation? Life is a voyage of endless discovery from which no man returns...Shakespeare reminds us that all the world's a stage and all the men and women are merely players. Although I plan to make acting my career, in my personal life I choose to be the hand and not the puppet; the director of my own destiny."

This was a hard act to follow. We were awestruck. Sue Cooper tried but came off very lamely; she claimed Miss Maxwell was her most fascinating acquaintance. Bunky Block made hideous kissing sounds when she finished. The rest of us sat on our hands. I did not offer to read my tribute to the realtor/chiropractor.

Rosella and I walked home after school. I hoped Raymond might join us but he had a drama club meeting. Rosella tried to hide a small smile of relief.

It was a sharp, fine autumn afternoon. A cloudburst had washed away the gravel truck dust, leaving the evergreens and the deep lawns clean and lush. The sun ignited Mrs. Phillips' poplars. They burned like yellow spears.

We passed Kumquat National Bank as its president stepped out the door.

"Girls," he said accurately, tipping an imaginary hat. "Olivia, may I speak with you for a moment?"

"Sure."

He rolled on his heels, uncertain how to begin, then plunged in. "Olivia, I know this isn't the best bank in the world, but it's certainly not the worst bank."

"No, sir." -

"No, sir; not by a long shot. It's just as good as the bank in Cedar. Why doesn't Luna Lee bank here anymore?"

"I beg your pardon?"

"She never makes deposits; only withdrawals. And I tell you, Liv, what goes up must come down. What goes out must come in. In other words, at the current rate, that account will be emptied by—"

"—next July."

"That's right, just about the time you finish school. Now, I understand your mother's working in Cedar. I heard she was in sales. Or a restaurant hostess. Or a cab driver, for heaven's sake! You can't believe the nonsense you hear in this town."

"No, sir. There's always a lot of nonsense going around."

He nodded grimly. "I understand that our hours aren't the most convenient, but this is your classic chicken-or-the-egg situation: Increased business equals increased banking hours. We can't do it alone."

"No, you can't."

"No, we can't. Convenience is important, of course, but it can never hold a candle to loyalty and tradition. Your family has always banked at Kumquat National—" He consulted his watch and cut it short. "—And I hope you'll continue with us for years to come. Good day, girls."

"Good day," we chorused.

"You never mentioned your mother was driving a cab," Rosella said.

"She could be, for all I know." It made a strange picture in my mind: Mother at the wheel, brazen and brave, blazing through traffic. Mother never drove.

Rosella went home. She and her mother were going

shopping for blouses and skirts. Every fall all the girls go shopping with their mothers, filling me with longing for a time I never knew. Mother and I seldom did mother/daughter things like that. She didn't like to leave the house, or go out of town, and her fashion sense was undependable. She was apt to pick clothes several years out of date, or clothes too old for me; clothes just right for her romance novel heroines. Mother always thought I was older than I was. She was right.

I wasn't ready to go home and be alone, so I went to the library, located in a cozy little house donated by the American Legion.

"Greetings, Olivia!"

"Hello, Mrs. Wallis."

Mrs. Wallis, the librarian, is a pale, pretty woman with dark red lipstick and smooth brown hair. A long time ago there was a Mr. Wallis. He came through town selling space-age appliances, and Mrs. Wallis (the former Genevieve Simpson) married him at the Methodist Church and left town with him. Like that. Three months later she was back, alone. No one knows what happened but everyone speculates.

I like Mrs. Wallis very much and she likes me. Sometimes, when we talk about the true loves of her life—the NASA program and science fiction novels—she gets so excited her hands fly and her gray eyes fill with tears—and she turns her head away. Her gaze is firm and dry when she looks back at me, and we silently agree it didn't happen. Again.

"Winter's coming. It's getting dark early." She lit the green-shaded lamp on her desk. The only other person in the library was Mr. Burch. He's too cheap to subscribe to the *Messenger,* so he comes in once a week to catch up.

"Olivia, I have the most wonderful book for you!"

Mrs. Wallis produced yet another thick volume of science fiction. Frankly, I can't get too enthused. Life is strange enough; I don't need to go to Mars for amazement. Mrs. Wallis, on the other hand, spends as much time as possible in outer space.

"I know you'll enjoy it. It has the most intricate plot. And the heroine absolutely bristles with vitality! Would you like to check it out?"

"Well, I . . . have a lot of reading for school."

The light in her shiny eyes flickered and dimmed.

"But yes, I'd love to read it."

"Good." Mrs. Wallis took my library card. Then, carefully arranging her mouth, she said, "How is your mother these days?"

"Just fine."

Mrs. Wallis stifled a sigh. She has never approved of Mother and once told me that I had too many responsibilities for such a young girl. This was shortly after Mother left, and the mailbox fell over, and Mrs. Wallis drove by while I was sinking the pole into fresh cement.

She also told me she wished she had a daughter just like me, and I was so lonesome that day I almost told her I was available. She means well, but she couldn't have kept my secret; she wouldn't have understood. Just as I have never understood why she came back to Kumquat after Mr. Wallis left her, or she left him, depending on who's telling the story. (Some rumors concerning the mythical Mr. Wallis: he was a rambler, a gambler, a bigamist, a homosexual, a mobster, a flim-flam man on the lam, or all of the above. At one Founder's Day Barbecue the pharmacist's wife asked her point-blank what happened to Mr. Wallis. Mrs. Wallis reportedly "blanched, turned absolutely chalk white" and refused to discuss it.)

Funny, all the secrets in people's lives. We're icebergs, only the tip of us showing. I'm an iceberg, too. I'm the biggest liar in town. Someday they'll discover that Mother is gone, and they'll realize I've told a hundred million lies and the person they thought they knew so well has been a stranger all along.

"Going home, Liv?" asked Mr. Burch, following Mrs. Wallis's lengthy and utterly baffling synopsis of the book now tucked under my arm.

"Yes, Mr. Burch."

"Could you drop me off?"

"I walked."

He frowned and abruptly departed. He has two cars but he's too tight to spring for gas. When he dies, he'll stuff himself into a jumbo trash bag and set himself out on the curb.

"I'm glad you came by, Olivia. I know you'll enjoy the book."

"I'm sure I will," I told Mrs. Wallis.

"I don't suppose—" She shook her head. "No, it's such short notice. I was wondering if you might come for supper tonight, but your mother must be expecting you."

"She said she had to work late."

Mrs. Wallis looked delighted. "Would you care to join me in a bowl of soup?"

"Do you think there'll be room for both of us?"

Mrs. Wallis looked confused but she smiled politely. "It's vegetable. It's homemade."

"Sounds great."

She beamed. She clasped her silky hands. "We'll stop by the market and get some French bread, the round, crusty kind. It makes the house smell so good!"

She hummed as she buzzed around the library, locking it for the night. Joy rose in me, yeasty and warm. I was humming my father's song.

6

I sit on the dark porch, the mail in my lap. I've finally had a postcard from Mother. The picture on the front shows a sleek porpoise diving through a flaming hoop, beneath the big red words SAN DIEGO! That's close— at least, it's closer than Montana.

Honey!
This is in a hurry cuz the bus leaves in five secs & I
don't want it leaving without me. You should see me—
I'm so tan from the beach! The sand is as soft and white
as macaroni (cooked). There are lots of sailors here,
they look like little boys. I hope you liked the necklace!
See you soon!

Love, Mother

Where was the bus going? What was Mother's destination? And who was this brown stranger bursting with exclamations? The old Mother was as pale as, well, as macaroni, cooked or uncooked, and her sentences tended to fade away . . .

She could walk through the door any second. Mother will come back to Kumquat someday. Or maybe, like the necklace she sent, she'll be lost along the way.

I always think I want to get a postcard from Mother, but they leave me sad and restless, like before a storm when the barometer falls. When I hear from Mother I remember she's real, and I miss her most. She's not a dream.

The rest of the mail was unexciting: a catalogue of overpriced dresses, a flat phone bill (who would I call?), a flyer from the pharmacy, and my order of bumper stickers.

A vise grips me nights when the moon is down and the wind is wild—I love the wind, stirring all it touches, invisible yet no one denies it exists. Darkly dressed, I glide down the street; helpless to fight this unbounded urge, this odious obsession, this pathetic perversion— that's how they talk in Mother's romance books—this BUMPER STICKER MADNESS.

I started three years ago when I came across a bumper sticker booth at the flea market in Cedar. One sticker screamed out to be taped (for painless removal; I do have my scruples) on the back of Mr. Burch's Rambler: CAPITALISM SUCKS! SHARE THE WEALTH! He drove around town all day before he discovered it, leaving the sidewalk talkers in stitches.

Three months later the Mayor's pickup truck invited other drivers to HONK IF YOU HAVE A HICKEY!

I don't overdo it. I don't know *why* I do it. I like being out at night, slipping through the shadows. And it gives everybody a laugh.

If I were a psychiatrist I'd say it was weird but harmless. I'd say I was waiting for the other shoe to drop. To be caught: for the School Board or the Police Chief or my Uncle Sargent to break down the door: "Come quietly, Liv. The jig is up."

I go over and over and over it in my mind. Why am I in this weird situation? Why did Mother leave me? I've always believed that she went for the margarine, with no other plan in mind, but that something about the evening sky, or the breeze, or the smell of waking winter, moved her as nothing ever had.

I've always believed that her exit surprised her as much as it did me. On the other hand, it's possible that she made a decision; that she put on her plaid coat and walked out the door with the waiting Greyhound firmly in mind. All planned.

Nope. Mother never planned, and she never lied. She didn't know how; it would've confused her. The truth was already too complicated.

I remember when she took up smoking. She did it because the people in her romance books were always lounging around, puffing at each other.

Grandmother was appalled. She hated smoking, hated everything about it; the smell, the results, the ashes all over the rugs, the idea that Mother paid good money for something she then burned up.

At first, because it was Mother, Grandmother tried the subtle approach, marching through the house with a wand of pine-scented air freshener, all the while shooting Mother looks that would've killed the average person. Our house smelled like a national forest. Mother never noticed. There was so much she never noticed.

One night the three of us watched a strange Italian movie, where gladiators moved their lips for ten minutes while a dubbed-in voice with a New York accent said, "Okay, Spartacus. See you later."

Mother was draped on the couch, smoking. This was during the period when she wore her hair parted way over on one side, so that it swooped dramatically across her eyes, deflecting Grandmother's gaze, which was boring into her head.

Grandmother's restraint amazed me. She was usually the essence of pith, believing fancy footwork was foolish when a right cross to the jaw worked just as well.

Finally she couldn't stand it anymore. As the Italians swarmed in their short skirts, she said: "Luna Lee, why are you smoking? You don't even inhale."

"Inhale?" Mother said.

"On your cigarette."

"On my cigarette?" Mother repeated with a gentle smile, as though Grandmother had suddenly lost her mind. "What do you mean?"

Grandmother's eyes bulged as if she'd been slapped. Mother's lack of sophistication always shocked her, but this time she'd hit a new high.

"I mean take the smoke into your lungs! Inhale!"

Mother was astonished. "I didn't know you could do that! I thought you were supposed to fill your mouth with smoke and blow it out."

She wasn't a dumbbell. It simply wasn't in her nature to think up or do unnatural things. But she gave it a try, gamely filling her lungs, then turning her horrified face to us. Grandmother talked her out of throwing up.

Mother stopped smoking, along with the heroines of her novels, who changed with the times and took up jogging. She never jogged; she thought of her body as a party dress that could be tattered by too much activity. But she enjoyed reading about people who jogged; it made her feel strong and healthy. That was a happy time for Mother. Her heroines were doing exciting things. They were glamorous and powerful and ambitious and sleek.

She liked to describe the plots of these novels at the dinner table. This drove Grandmother silently wild. For one thing, the plots were remarkably similar, and for another, Mother would jump up and act out the dialogue: "It's true that I love you, Edwin, but I have my own life to live!"; knocking over water glasses and vases. I didn't mind. I liked to see her happy. Grandmother liked that too. She loved Mother and tried to protect her. Sometimes, when she looked at Mother, those clear, fierce eyes turned cloudy. She must have wondered what would happen to us after she was gone. She must have wondered how it had come to this: a vanished husband, her only child dead, a daughter-in-law in dreamland, and an odd, close-mouthed grandkid. Strange as it was, our life was all I had ever known. I never imagined another life but I expect Grandmother did.

It's different now. She's gone, Mother too. Sometimes I feel like I'll explode with being alone; that I'll die, truly die, if someone doesn't hug me.

I'm afraid I'll pick up the phone and scream: Help me, somebody! Help me.

Then, as clearly as if she were beside me, I hear Grandmother's sensible voice: *Worse things happen at sea, Olivia. Everyone's alone inside their skin.*

I'm sitting on the porch swing, Mother, thinking of you. Are you thinking of me? I'm wondering where you are and when I'll see you again, and I'm wondering what we'll say to each other.

And I'm thinking about Grandmother and my father, the mystery man; and about all the people in the world I'll never know, and all the people who have ever lived;

millions of them, swept away, who laughed and loved and wondered and wept...

And I'm thinking about the stars, and how far away they are, and how long it takes their little lights to reach me.

7

I went to the Halloween dance with Raymond.

Rosella decided to stay home.

"Wait and see," she said. "He'll go as Dracula."

"Gude eve-a-ning," he said when I opened the door. He was breathtaking in his black clothes and black cape, his long hair slicked back, his eyes hollow with painted shadows. Plastic fangs tipped his eyeteeth. Delicate beads of blood trickled from the corners of his mouth.

"Raymond, you look fantastic!"

"Thanks. Aren't you going to wear a costume?"

"This *is* my costume." I was going as a hobo, but next to Raymond, who'd notice?

When we got to the school gym, the band was blasting. We almost turned back at the door. Bunky Block's drums sounded like they were strapped to his feet and an angry mob was chasing him.

The gym was quite dark, a triumph for the dance committee. The school board had wanted the room fully lit. "Fully lit!" Bunky protested at the school board meeting. "Why doncha have searchlights and armed guards and make the couples dance five feet apart?"

Two board members thought this sounded fine, but darkness prevailed. The stage, however, was splashed with spotlights, in case someone wanted to chuck something at the band.

Raymond took my arm and we began to stroll.

People were shocked by his appearance; so tall and thin, his skin so white, almost violet in the flash of the strobe lights. There's something about Raymond that draws people's eyes, even when he's not disguised as Dracula.

Merry materialized, dressed as a rag doll, her freckled cheeks painted pink. "Having a good time, Liv?" She snuck a peek at Raymond. Merry is suffocating with a crush on him; when he's around she can barely speak. The other day she told me she was sorry, that she couldn't help how she felt. I assured her Raymond and I are just friends. She practically collapsed with relief.

We stood together for a moment talking, then Raymond steered me onto the dance floor.

The top of my head brushed his chin. His arms wrapped around me twice.

"Having fun?" he whispered so close to my ear the words seemed to come from my mind.

"Yes, but Raymond . . ."

"What?"

"You're strangling me."

"What can you expect from a vampire?" He laughed and held me just as close.

He's odd, so different at different times; funny one minute, then moody and withdrawn. He worries about his father; there's no hiding from the mob, so Big Ray is supposed to look retired. He does, spending most of his time playing lowball at Danny's Inferno.

We left after he won the costume contest. He said the dance was too rinkydink. On the way back to his house he told me about the school dances in Los Angeles. They were held in the ballrooms of fancy hotels. The girls wore formals and the boys wore tuxedos. Raymond would sure look handsome all dressed up.

Mr. and Mrs. Mooney and Sophronia were watching TV. The mini-Mooneys had been dispatched to their rooms, where they were devouring their Halloween candy. Mrs. Mooney said I looked very cute. Mr. Mooney and Sophronia didn't speak.

Raymond took off his cape and black boots. We drank coffee at the kitchen table. He talked about the kids at our school; how young and thick and dumb they are compared to his friends in Los Angeles. I said I thought the kids at our school are all right. He said, "That's because you've never been out of town."

"Have you ever been in love, Liv?"

He caught me unprepared. "You mean loved somebody besides my family?"

Raymond looked pained. He either acts like I'm the only other intelligent person around or a prize fool.

"Of course I mean besides your family. I mean love."

"No," I answered truthfully. "Have you?"

He stood and poured himself another cup of coffee. I

wanted some too, but he forgot to ask, and the look on his face stopped me.

"Yes," he said, frowning into his cup. "A woman in Los Angeles."

I waited. The silence stretched until it ticked.

"You would've liked her, Liv. Everybody did," Raymond blurted. "She was so beautiful. She was so pretty! On the inside, too, where it really counts. She was the nicest person I've ever known."

"You must've hated to leave her."

"I didn't leave her. She died."

His words froze in the air.

"Raymond, I'm so sorry—"

"It's okay." He waved away my apology. "I can talk about it now." He picked up a spoon and stirred his coffee, stirred it round and round. "She was twenty years old. We were just like this." He entwined two fingers. "I was with her when she died. I was always at her house. Her family was so great. Her mom told me later how happy I'd made Holly, and how much they'd all hoped—" He stopped, his face tight. "It didn't work out the way we'd hoped. There aren't enough miracles to go around."

I had to say something. "How did you meet her?"

Raymond smiled fondly, remembering. "At an audition. Holly was a wonderful actress. She would've been a legend if she'd lived . . . We were going to have the most fantastic life together! We were going to get married and move to New York, so we could hone our craft on the stage. Holly said we'd be the new Lunts."

"The who?"

He looked disgusted. "Only the most famous couple in the history of the theater!"

"I'm sorry. I didn't know."

He sighed. "Of course you didn't. I didn't mean to

snap at you. It's just that—I still can't believe it really happened! One day Holly felt a little tired. She got tireder and tireder—I told her to go to the doctor! By the time she did—two months later she was gone! Gone! How the hell could she be gone like that? She was so alive, so full of life!" He shook his head, his face twisted. "Holly was . . . I'll show you her picture sometime. She was gorgeous, right to the end. Her hair was even longer than yours, and her eyes were so blue, they got bluer and bluer—I'm sorry." Raymond touched my wrist. "I didn't mean to get so depressing."

"That's okay." I ached for Raymond. I knew exactly how he felt. When you lose people you love, you always miss them. The loss doesn't diminish. The pain doesn't fade. You keep it at bay, behind a closed door, but when you open the door, it's there.

"I never talk about her to anyone," Raymond said. "People act too scared or embarrassed. But I *have* to talk to someone, Liv! I feel like I'm going to explode! I don't want to forget her! She was too important!"

"You have to talk to someone," I agreed, knowing that I would've withered without Rosella. Rosella. We hadn't studied in days. I'd been busy with Raymond. I would call her tomorrow.

Then Raymond described Holly in such loving detail I could almost see her, too. Her favorite color was yellow. Her breath was sweet as vanilla. Children and puppies flocked around her. When she smiled, people always smiled back.

They planned to marry after Raymond graduated from Pasadena Playhouse. As important as their careers would be, family would always come first. They would have two children, Jeremy and Jenny. Maybe twins; there were twins in Holly's family. Wouldn't that be something, two babies for the price of one!

Then Raymond remembered that there wouldn't be any babies. Holly was gone forever.

Tears filmed his eyes. "I have to talk about her, Liv. I can't let her fade away! And if I try to talk to Ma, she gets so weepy and tragic, and the kids—I can't talk to the kids."

"I'm glad you talk to me, Raymond, I am."

"Thank you." He squeezed my hand.

Mrs. Mooney bustled in, yawning hugely. It was time for me to go home. Raymond drove me in the Mooney-mobile, a beat-up old station wagon big as a hearse.

He parked in front of my house, his face halved; one side moonlit, the other shadowed. His eyes were on me but his gaze was distant, as though he looked at something far away.

"When you love someone, you never lose them," I said. "You keep them in your heart."

"I know, but I need to touch her!" he whispered. "I need to see her face!"

How could I comfort Raymond? I knew the feeling, not the cure.

"Well, he said. "I better let you go. Thanks for listening."

"That's what friends are for."

Tenderly cupping my face in his hands, he pressed his lips to my forehead.

I stood on the porch, watching him drive away, aching for the hurt he had known. My heart was swollen with memories, swollen with condolences that left me empty. My heart, like my house, was full of ghosts.

8

If I had to be stuck on a desert island with one person, I'd choose Rosella. She has the grace to be close without crowding.

When I honked the horn, she bounced out to the car and didn't ask where I'd been keeping myself, or why I hadn't called. She said, "How was the dance?" and I said, "Fine," and we skated across the thin ice of Raymond, into the Saturday morning.

The Plymouth purred, the radio worked and the deep blue sky floated marshmallow clouds. Autumn was Grandmother's favorite season. She thought spring naive and summer overdone, but she cherished fall's ripeness, that perfect moment balanced on the brink of winter. I love the fall, too. I love all the seasons. Humming down the highway with Rosella, I was happy.

The flea market in Cedar was well underway when we arrived. It's a weekly event, cheerfully frantic, a jungle of loot and junk. If you're hunting treasure you have to dive deep, through piles of velvet Elvis paintings, seashell ashtrays, splintered kitchen chairs, golden lockets, clothes laundered lifeless, feather earrings, dented pots and pans, chewed-on kids' books, sequined evening bags, bikes, tools, toys, tires and freshly stolen stereo equipment, sold by men with bottle cap eyes, from the back of bashed-up vans.

I love the antiques; the old postcards and valentines, the faded family portraits in their heavy carved frames, the stiff high-necked dresses and the silk and paper fans, delicate as butterfly wings.

We browsed from booth to booth, scouting for bargains and good books. At lunchtime we lugged a stack of paperbacks out to the car, then sat at one of the picnic tables to eat tostadas and hot apple pie.

The breeze was chilly but the food and coffee warmed us. We laughed, getting silly, delighted with each other and relieved that we weren't fighting. I'd forgotten how good it felt to be with Rosella, how her eyes gleam when she's going to say something funny. She'll call my attention to someone going by, starring in the private play of their life, like that man over there in the ten-gallon hat and the cowboy boots with such pointed toes they could puncture tomato juice cans—and she'll make a quiet observation, not cruel, only true...There's not much Rosella misses.

When Mother first left and my life became peculiar, I wondered how I'd tell if I went crazy. This worried me. Living alone, it would be easy to get stranger and stranger, never realizing that you'd fallen off the world outside your door.

With Rosella for my friend, I was never really alone. When I got lost, she called my name. People go crazy when they wander off the beaten path and nobody calls them back.

That's kind of what happened with Mother. But she didn't go crazy—she simply went. She was elusive even when present, real as a shimmering soap bubble. Grandmother and I always held our breath, fearful she would burst.

Silly us. She's made of stronger stuff than we ever expected. Mother's bouncing all over the nation like a rubber ball.

Rosella finished my coffee. "How's Mama Spider?"

"Fine. You should see the size of her web. It's amazing."

"That thing's going to cover the whole house someday."

"Great. I can charge admission."

"Not from me. Spiders bug me."

"They serve a useful purpose," I insisted. "They eat flies."

"What purpose do flies serve?"

"Spiders eat them. And don't forget maggots."

"Who could forget maggots?"

Mama Spider is large and velvet black, with beautiful yellow markings. Her web occupies one corner of the parlor, draping the bay window like the finest Irish lace.

How did she learn to embroider those designs? She does what she was born to do. Her web is more intricate than any antimacassar and as strong as it is fragile. Riding the breeze from the open window, it billows, never tearing.

We looked around after lunch. The bumper sticker man was there but his merchandise was tacky.

"Tacky! You call that tacky?" Rosella said. "What about 'Honk If You Have A Hernia!'?"

"On the mayor's truck? It was 'Hickey.'"

"That's class."

"Well, the mayor's a classy guy. Anyway, I order most of my stickers through the mail now."

"You better hope the mailman never finds out. He'll

have it all over town faster than the twenty-four-hour flu."

"They come in a plain brown wrapper, like me. You're talking to the mystery woman."

Rosella said, "Speaking of mystery women, what do you hear from Luna Lee?"

"I got a postcard last week," I said, "from San Diego. She said she has a great tan and she'll see me soon."

"How soon?"

"She didn't say." I examined a remarkably ugly lamp, its shade encrusted with glossy seashells that looked like painted toenails.

"She'll come back," Rosella promised. "She'll come back someday."

"By then it will be too late!" I walked away. "I won't need a mother! I'll be on my own!"

"You're on your own now."

"You know what I mean."

"You know what *I* mean, too," she said.

We walked without talking, the crowd rippling around us.

"You don't have to need her to love her. She's your mother," Rosella said.

"She sure doesn't act like a mother!"

"I know, but that's how she is."

"That's no excuse!" My voice was too loud. "Why does my family have to be so damn *weird*? Weird? That's a laugh! They're dead or gone. All I've got left are my adorable uncle and aunt, Mr. and Mrs. Piranha, and their equally repulsive children. Not to mention my grandparents, who pretend I don't exist. Those people aren't my family! Where is my family? I can't be a family by myself!"

Rosella didn't say anything. She looked at me and listened, her brown eyes warm and calm as cocoa.

"It's funny, you know, Rosella? In a way, it's like

they're still alive. I mean real and in my life. I hear
Grandmother's voice, giving me advice. I know how
she'd handle each situation . . . And the old guys on the
bench downtown talk about my father like he's still
around: 'Remember the time he cartwheeled down the
bar?' My father still makes them smile . . . And everybody tells me to say hi to Mother, and we have these
crazy conversations: 'Yes, Mother's fine. She's a rhumba
instructor in Cedar. I'll tell her you've been meaning to
call. Yes, we're all pretty busy these days . . .'

"It's hard to remember what's real, sometimes. Sometimes what's real isn't nearly as nice as something you
make believe. You make it up, but you believe it, too;
because you want to, or maybe you *have* to."

I stopped, embarrassed, in the present. People were
packing up their booths and going home. We drifted
toward the parking lot.

Rosella said, "I wish I were magic, Liv. I'd fix things."

"No one said life was fair."

"Sure they did! When we were kids, the teacher told
us we had to take turns; no pushing, no shoving, no
cutting in line. If somebody cheated, we all screamed:
'That's not fair!' and the cheater had to go to the end of
the line. But in *real* life—" Rosella's eyes widened
"—you discover that people not only cut in line, they
push and shove and bite and scratch, so they can take
more turns than anyone else . . . Not all people," she
added softly. "But it's different than I expected."

Looking at Rosella I remembered she is black; something she never forgets. I'll never know exactly how the
world looks to her eyes, nor will she know how my life
feels to me. Our colors don't come between us; it's our
skin. We're as close as two separate creatures can be.

Sometimes I wish I were so close to someone they
would wrap around me like a quilt, and I'd never feel

separate or lonely or cold, and being alive would never frighten me again.

Don't make an opera out of it, Liv, Grandmother would say. *That's life. Get on with living.*

All the way home the Eternal Deejay played our favorite songs. We soared along the highway, high as the silver arrows of Canada geese.

As I dropped off Rosella, her mother opened the front door and waved.

"We want you to come for supper soon, Livvy. We're on our way to John's tonight," she called. John is Rosella's older brother.

"How about tomorrow?" Rosella suggested. "We'll have supper before we study."

"Study?"

"We always study on Sunday night, remember?"

I slapped my forehead. "I know. I forgot. Raymond asked me to go to the movies."

"No problem." Rosella got out of the car.

"I can call him and cancel—"

"It's no big deal." She leaned in the window. "We can study Monday night."

"Sure. Or Tuesday. He said something about Monday."

"Whenever. Give me a call," she said.

"I really feel terrible about tomorrow."

"Relax. I'm not crossing you off my Christmas card list."

"I know, but—"

"Things don't stay the same," Rosella said.

"What things?"

"Things change."

"Not me," I said.

"Why not? You can't help it."

I said, "Is this conversation getting weird, or is it me?"

"It's both of us," Rosella said. "See you at school."

"I'll call him and cancel—"

"No." She shook her head. "It's fine. I'm just tired tonight, that's all. I'll see you on Monday."

"You sure?"

"I'm sure!" She thumped the hood and waved me along. Her smile seemed to go all the way to her eyes. Why did I feel there was something wrong?

I watched her recede in the rearview mirror, shrinking until she disappeared. The golden day faded like a photograph I might be looking at, years later, remembering Rosella.

9

I do all my errands every Monday after school. Raymond thinks that's ridiculous; he says I should be more spontaneous. He says if I'm like this at seventeen, imagine how I'll be by thirty. There's such a thing as too much organization, he says. You have to open the door and let life barge right in!

He doesn't know that life has barged in daily, ever since Mother barged out.

First, I went by the bank to get some money. Bunky Block's sister, Doris, waited on me.

"You sure look cute today, Liv. That blouse is darling. Seems like you're taller every time you come in. What size shoe are you wearing now?"

"Eight."

"Eight! I bet you're bigger than your mother! She's such a teeny little thing, with those big blue eyes bugging out—not bugging. Prominent. You know what I mean. How *is* Luna Lee? Seems like ages since I've seen her. Time sure flies. One minute it's summer, now all the kids are back in school. Bunky's graduating this spring! Can you believe that?"

"No."

"I'll tell you something else amazing: I've finished all my Christmas shopping! I'm so proud of myself! Did you need something, Liv?"

"Just that check cashed."

"Twenty, forty, sixty, eighty. Don't spend it all in one place."

"I won't."

We say that every Monday, except for legal holidays, in which event we say it on Tuesday.

At the pharmacy I bought Vitamin C. I take C and a multivitamin and I'm hardly ever sick. I bought myself a Swiss chocolate bar and chocolate laced with orange for Rosella and a wand of Mother's favorite lipstick. The pharmacist's wife waited on me. She was wearing a grape-jelly colored skirt and sweater set.

"Here are your mother's books. Oh, this is a good

one. It's sad, you know, but it's happy, too. Did you mention those cards to your mother?''

"Cards?''

"Remember, I told you we got our Christmas cards in, and I thought Luna Lee might like to take a look.''

"She did,'' I said. "She bought a box of the Santas in scuba gear.''

"Really? I must've missed her. Oh, it was probably while I was at Sorority. Which reminds me: I'm having a Tupperware party at the house Wednesday night. You and Luna Lee are invited.''

"Thanks, but we already have a ton of Tupperware.''

"There's no such thing as too much, Liv,'' she said. "You should start your own collection. Merry started hers when she turned thirteen, and I do think it's important for mothers and daughters to do things together.''

This was a veiled reference to the school's recent Mother–Daughter Senior Tea, which, needless to say, we missed.

"Tell her the party starts at seven-thirty and we're going to have refreshments and a door prize, too.''

"I'll tell her but she might have to work that night.''

"Rush, rush, rush,'' the pharmacist's wife sighed. "That's the tragedy of modern life. Where does all that hurrying get us? A hundred years from now what difference will it make?''

"Good question,'' I said, when I could think of no answer.

"Seven-thirty,'' she said. "Don't forget.''

I stopped by the post office for stamps.

"How's it going, Liv?'' the postmaster inquired.

"Pretty good, and you?''

"Can't complain but I do.'' He grinned. "Your mother ever straighten out that thing with *McCall's*?''

For several months she received three copies of every issue.

"Yes, finally. I don't know what the problem was."

"The problem is those damn computers," he said. "You can't reason with a machine."

"That's the truth."

I stopped by the library to return the science fiction book, which was so completely confusing it might've been written in Martian. Mrs. Wallis was reading a magazine at her desk, but she spoke as soon as I entered, as if she'd been awaiting my arrival.

"Olivia, do you believe there is some truly Divine plan for humanity, or do you think we simply ricochet from one day to the next? I sometimes feel as though we're lost in a dark woods, following a shining trail of bread crumbs. But are the crumbs Divine, or do we toss them ourselves?"

There was a brief pause while I stared at her and she stared at a spot just beyond me.

"You ought to read this article, Olivia. It raises some interesting points."

Out of the corner of my eye I spied two members of the Deer Ridge church slipping books under their coats and slipping out the door. The books were from the anatomy section.

"Mrs. Wallis, those people—"

"I know, dear." She sighed. "I've spoken to them before. They feel those books are a bad influence. I'm sure Jesus wouldn't agree. I plan to take appropriate action, as soon as I determine what that might be. Did you enjoy the science fiction?"

"You were right, it was really intricate."

"Then I know you'll love this one. It just came in." She produced a fat volume. "*The Aphids of Angkar.*

The author draws the most amazing parallels between these insects' lives and our life here on Earth.''

"Great.''

At Watson's Market I instinctively chose the cart with the most rattly wheels. I navigated it up and down the narrow aisles, filling it with two cartons of milk, a dozen eggs, cottage cheese, bananas, apples, kumquats, potatoes, salad greens, pork chops, chicken, peanut butter, rye bread, dish detergent, English muffins, binder paper, Hershey kisses and split pea soup.

Ruthie Ray rang me up.

"Can you believe these pork chops? The cost of meat? I'll have to start cooking up the kids,'' she said. "Hey, Liv, how come you're such a good kid and I've got all those meatballs at home? You're always doing errands, always helping out your mom—''

"I like doing the shopping,'' I said.

"Don't worry, you'll get over that. That's how I felt when me and Lou got married. I thought I was playing house.'' She weighed the plastic bag of kumquats. "Are these any good?''

"If you like kumquats.''

"They're sure expensive. Do you peel off the skin or do you eat the whole thing?''

"You eat the whole thing. They're kind of sweet and sour.''

"For that price they ought to be big and sweet. Here's your receipt, hon. Have a good day.''

As I drove home the sky darkened, filling with dramatic black clouds. Home, this huge, brooding, ivy-covered hulk. The red leaves had fallen off, revealing the web of veins. In a way, it looks like a horror-movie house; the kind of house where the closets eat you and the stairs are razor blades. Screaming, the heroine runs from room to room. At last! She finally escapes!...Only to remember she forgot her purse: it's inside, on the kitchen table. *Don't go back in there, you fool!* She always does. *What's the matter with her, is she crazy?*

No, she lives there. I carried in the groceries, then went out to check the mailbox.

There was a circular from Sears, a catalogue of spring bulbs, a chance to win one million dollars, and a small pink envelope. My heart lurched; it was probably from my aunt and uncle, demanding that we celebrate Thanksgiving together. This was like spending Halloween with Jack the Ripper. I reluctantly ripped it open and read:

> *My dearest Liv,*
> *Please forgive me.*
> *I wouldn't blame you if you don't, and if you never want to see me again, or if you don't even bother to read this letter. (I hope you do.) I just want you to understand I had NO INTENTION OF DESERTING YOU.*
> *Remember, I went out for margarine that night. The sky was silver and the clouds were pink, and the wind was like something alive, something dancing.*
> *You know how you feel like a kite sometimes, when the wind fills you up and you sail away? Maybe you don't know what I mean, Livvy. You were always so down to earth.*
> *That night, for the first time, I felt as though my life, MY life, was full of infinite possibilities, infinite as the stars and the wind, as though I could walk forever, or maybe even fly—*
> *The next thing I knew, I was in Truth or Consequences, New Mexico, at the Greyhound Station coffee counter. I was so confused. I had no suitcase, of course; only my purse and a pound of margarine. In order to make ends meet, I got a waitressing job for forty-five minutes. (There was an incident involving a bowl of Cream of Wheat but I won't bore you with details.)*

BELIEVE ME, LIV: I PLANNED TO COME BACK RIGHT AWAY. But I could never seem to get headed in that direction. Things came up. Things got in the way. Not that I'm making excuses: this whole thing is ALL MY FAULT.

So many times I wished you were with me. So many times I almost called. But after a while I was afraid to; I was afraid you'd hang up when you heard my voice.

I hope these past few months haven't been awful. I know you've been taking good care of yourself. You were always so much smarter than Daddy and me. Wait and see, I'll make it up to you! And remember: MY LEAVING HAD NOTHING TO DO WITH YOU AND EVERY-THING TO DO WITH ME. It sounds so selfish and awful but it's true. I didn't know I was going until I was gone.

And though I hope you'll forgive me, I won't blame you if you tell me to get lost forever. (I hope you don't.) In the meantime, I hope you like this little necklace. It's got a heart of gold just like you.

I'm coming home, Liv. I really mean it.

Love forever, Mother

My mind went blind, went blank, went reeling; joy, rage, hurt, hope roiling into one enormous feeling. What would I do when I finally saw Mother; hug her, or punch her in the nose? Which first?

I went into the house. I blew from room to room, touching curtains, lampshades, chairs, thinking how they would look to Mother; placing her vinyl autograph hound, with the blue tattoos of her schoolmates' names, more firmly on the middle of her bed.

I'm coming home, Liv.

I was laughing and crying. It was crazy! Mother would slide back into Kumquat and no one would ever realize she'd been gone. People would say, "Luna Lee, it's been ages!'' and Mother would agree, marveling at how quickly these "past few months" had flown.

Mother's coming back! Can it really be true? What will it be like to have her home again? She sounds so different from the Mother I remember; older and more *real*. I'm older, too.

I reread the letter. I watched out the window. I turned on the porch light, nutty with excitement, as if she were returning that second.

Mother could come back any second. She could float in the door like she floated away.

I remembered the necklace; it was still in the envelope, lying on the front lawn. I touched the tiny heart and fastened the filament around my throat; a fragile, shining chain connecting Mother and me.

This was the necklace she had mentioned in her postcard; the necklace I had thought was lost in the mail. How old was the letter? It wasn't dated.

The postmark on the envelope was six months old.

Six months ago she was in San Francisco. Six months ago she was five hours away. Mother wasn't coming back to Kumquat that day, or the next day, or the day after that. Like tomorrow, Mother never arrived.

Hope burst like a big balloon. A door closed deep inside me. Lost in my heart, a tiny child was weeping. Don't cry, I told her, don't be scared. You're not alone; you still have yourself. What hurts is the hope that you could have something else. Loneliness won't kill you, but it cuts like a knife, when it goes so deep down bone-lonely, to the place all the friendly strangers who know my face and my shoe size never reach.

I went back into the house. My feet led me upstairs, to Grandmother's room. It was just as she had left it; the bed neatly made, her belongings precisely arranged. Her ivory hair brush lay beside the row of perfume bottles. I dusted the furniture until it gleamed, then I opened the *White Shoulders* and inhaled her.

The walls of the room Mother shared with my father are painted jonquil yellow. They glowed in the pink light from the lamp on her nightstand. The bedspread was as smooth and inviting as new snow, but I knew if I lay down, I would never get up again.

On my father's bureau there is a picture of me and Mother, next to a small silver tray that holds his cuff links, tie tacks, house and car keys, and the good luck cat's-eye marble he always carried in his vest pocket. In the picture Mother is young and happy. I'm about two and I look like a marshmallow.

My father's suits hang in the closet. Mother's peignoir is on a hook behind the door.

Everything is ready and waiting, as if all three of them had just stepped out and will just as suddenly return.

They won't. I turned out the lights and went downstairs. I lit a fire in the parlor and ate my supper, then the kumquats. Only a fool seeks her sweet in the sour, again and again. I ate them all. Mama Spider hung motionless over my head, like a question mark, like a musical note.

That night I dreamed that Mother was a kite on the end of a long string I held in my hands. The wind made her dance; she went higher and higher. I tried to hold on but the string cut my flesh. It hurt too much. I had to let go. Mother disappeared, a tiny dot that got smaller and smaller and so far away that at last I wasn't looking at Mother; I was looking at where she'd been.

10

Raymond said, "What happened last night? You were supposed to call me." He was wearing a navy blue turtleneck sweater and looked very handsome, except for the frown.

"Aren't you going to ask me in?" He brushed past me into the parlor. "Incredible! The House of Usher. Look at the size of that spiderweb."

"Don't!" I leaped in alarm as he raised his arm.

"What is it, your pet?" Raymond regarded me as though he thought I was crazy but cute.

"Kind of."

"I'm surprised your grandmother puts up with it."

"Grandmother's dead. I thought you knew."

He was stunned. "I'm sorry. Why didn't you tell me?"

"I'm telling you now. There's not much to say."

"I know, but— Hey, not to change the subject, but do you have any coffee? I'm beat."

He sat at the kitchen table and watched me make the coffee.

"That's really too bad about your grandmother. She was a neat old lady, a tough old bird. Remember the time she found us playing doctor behind the barn? Boy, the look on her face almost fried my brain. Her eyes were kind of shooting sparks. Remember that, Liv?"

"Can't say as I do." I stuck my head in the fridge so he wouldn't see me blush.

"How come you weren't in school today?"

"I felt lousy this morning; kind of down."

"Maybe you're getting your period."

"Raymond!"

"No need to act embarrassed. It happens to lots of women. My mom cries and my sister acts psychotic, but she always acts psychotic, so it's hard to tell."

"Can we please change the subject? I feel fine now."

"You look terrific."

I had to turn away from his eyes. I glanced out the window above the kitchen sink. The framed view was in crayon colors: bright blue sky, vivid green grass, a red rag snapping on the clothesline. Another picture of the clothesline clicked into my mind: the empty arms of my father's white shirts, flapping like flags, embracing the sky.

"How's your mother?" Raymond asked.

"Fine."

"Pretty lady. You look a lot like her."

"Grandmother thought I looked like my father."

"Grandmother was wrong. Where's your mom?"

"At work," I said. "She's gone a lot, these days."

"You should get a dog to keep you company."

"I had a dog once. He ran away." I set our mugs of

coffee on the table and sat down. "Besides, I've got my spider."

Raymond smiled. "I like dogs. We had an English sheepdog, one of those big, fluffy, Walt Disney things. His name was Clancy."

"Did you have to give him away when you moved?"

"No." Raymond grimaced. "He was killed in the accident."

"What accident?"

"It's kind of hard to talk about, Liv."

"I'm sorry. I didn't mean to be so nosy."

Raymond ground a cookie into crumbs with his thumb. "It happened while Dad was with the Agency. We had this new car, a station wagon. It got great mileage for such a tank. And there was lots of room for the kids and Clancy." A shaft of sunlight speared the kitchen table. Raymond caught it in his hand.

"Anyway," he continued softly, "we were all going to the beach that day, coming down this mountain road. The brakes gave out. We were never sure why; we think the hydraulic lines were cut . . .

"Liv, you can't imagine what it was like in that car; the kids screaming and Ma crying and saying every prayer she knew. We were flying down that mountain, about an inch from the cliffs, but my dad never lost his cool. You should've seen him; he was steering like a champ. We never even nicked one other car.

"Then he shouted, 'Hold on!' and he drove into this bluff, and the car rolled over three times and finally stopped. 'Get out!' Daddy was yelling. 'Get them out of here, son!' He couldn't move; his leg was trapped."

Raymond took a deep drink of his coffee, wiping his mouth on the back of his hand. All the color had drained from his face and he spoke in a monotone. "I got Ma and the kids away from the car. Clancy wouldn't leave my dad. Ma always said he was loyal to a fault. That sure turned out to be the truth . . . Daddy's leg was broken; I yanked him out and dragged him. I was screaming for the dog: 'Come on, Clancy! Come on, boy!' But he was scared; he wouldn't move. I started back for him; Daddy stopped me. The next second that car exploded like a bomb, like a ball of flames.''

Raymond rubbed his eyes. "I should've saved Clancy."

"You did the best you could."

"No, I was too scared."

"For heaven's sake, Raymond! You saved their lives!"

"Not all their lives," he said. He gripped the empty mug so tightly his knuckles were bleached to the bone. I poured more coffee. His soft voice rose and fell as if he were recalling a dream.

"I used to take him for walks on the beach. He'd bark at the waves and chase the birds . . . The kids still dream about the dog. It's really sad. They have terrible nightmares, wake up screaming . . . And Dad's leg never healed right; you've probably noticed him favor it. I'm telling you all this because I trust you, Liv, and I want you to know the whole story. But it's top secret; nobody's supposed to know. And whatever you do, don't mention it to Ma. She hates this CIA stuff."

"So, you're all staying here until things cool off?"

"Exactly. After that, who knows? God, I can't *wait* to get out of this town! It's got the ambience of a gas station bathroom. Coming back here was an absolute disaster—except for you."

Raymond reached across the table and held one of my hands. The veins tingled up and down my arm. My blunt, unpolished fingernails looked raw next to his.

"Raymond, I have to tell you something—"

"Liv, I just want you to know where I stand. You don't have to feel the same way about me."

"It's about Mother," I gasped. I was sweating. My upper lip stuck to my teeth.

"What about her? You look so strange. Are you okay?"

"I have to tell you. She's—"

The phone rang.

"Let it ring," Raymond said.

I never let it ring. It might be Mother.

"Hi," Rosella said when I answered. "What's happening?"

"Not much."

"Are you feeling less depressed than you were this morning?"

"Yes."

"It sure doesn't sound like it."

"I'm fine," I insisted. "I'm just sitting here talking to Raymond."

Rosella said: "You didn't tell him about your mother, did you?"

"No, but—"

"Please don't tell him, Liv!" she begged. "Wait until you know it's safe!"

"Rosella, can we discuss this later?"

Raymond's hands were talking together, opening and closing like beaks. He held one beak up to his ear and listened.

"Wait until you know him better! If he tells on you, they'll send you away!"

"I'm not going anywhere," I said. "This whole situation is ridiculous. That letter yesterday was the frosting on the cake."

"I know how you feel, *but*—"

"No, you don't. *I* don't even know how I feel anymore. I'm sick of living on my own planet."

"You want Raymond to live there too?" she asked.

"Rosella, I'll have to call you back."

"Maybe I'll be here and maybe I won't."

"Suit yourself." I hung up the phone. I'd never hung up on Rosella before. I wanted to rush to her and make things right, but I wasn't even sure what was wrong.

"Sounds like you had a little hassle," Raymond said. "Don't worry, she'll get over it. It's perfectly natural for her to feel jealous; she thinks I'm muscling in on her territory. Sit down. You were going to tell me something."

I felt dazed. "It's not important."

"It's very important." He led me back to my chair. I drank more coffee. It was making me twitch. "Raymond, you have to keep this secret. Nobody knows about this but Rosella. You have to promise you'll never tell."

"Of course I won't. What's the problem, Liv?"

"Mother's gone." Hearing the words spoken aloud, I almost collapsed. I wanted to snatch them back.

"Gone where?"

"I don't know."

"I don't get it. You mean she's not at work?"

"I don't know where she is anymore," I said. "She's not at home."

Raymond shook his head. "I'm not following you, Liv. How long has she been gone?"

"Two years."

He almost fell out of his chair. "You haven't seen your mother for two years?"

"Two years this past September."

Raymond was in shock. "That's incredible. That's impossible."

"I know," I agreed, "but it's true."

"You've been by yourself all this time?" he spluttered. "How have you managed? How have you survived?"

"Grandmother left me some money," I said, "and I have that job with the *Messenger*."

"This is unbelievable." He couldn't stop shaking his head. "Why didn't you tell somebody she was gone?"

"I thought she'd be back," I said. "I was afraid she'd get in trouble. It's against the law to abandon your kid. And then...I didn't want to live with my uncle. That's a fate worse than death."

He was looking at me with astonished eyes, as though he'd never seen me before. "And for two years you've kept everyone from finding out she's gone?"

"Yes. Everyone but Rosella."

Raymond began to laugh as though this was the best joke he'd ever heard.

"It's not exactly a comedy situation."

"I know. I'm sorry." He covered his mouth. "It's just that the people in this town are so *dumb!* This whole damn thing is amazing!"

Then I told him what my life had been like and described the many useful things I'd learned to do. I told him that people don't listen long or well; when they ask how you are, they want you to say fine, so they can tell you how they're doing.

I told him about the forged signatures and the occasional impersonations over the phone.

I told him how much I hate secrets and lies.

It felt so good to tell the truth.

Raymond looked numb when I finished my story.

"Did you ever hear from your mother again?"

"Sure, I get a postcard now and then. I got a letter yesterday. She was on her way home."

"That's great!"

"It was written six months ago and got lost in the mail. She always says she's coming home. She never has, but you never know."

"That's the truth," he agreed incredulously. "Liv, don't you ever get lonely?"

"Yes," I said. "I get very lonely."

"Poor baby." His hand was on my arm. His eyes were huge and close. It struck me, suddenly, that Raymond was real, and that I was almost a grown-up woman and he was almost a grown-up man.

I jumped up and busied myself at the sink. "It's not so bad," I said. "Worse things happen at sea."

"That sounds like something your grandmother would say."

"She was right. What good does it do to feel sorry for yourself? It doesn't make things better."

"You don't have to be Superwoman with me," he said.

That made me very angry. I wanted to shout: *You don't know what it's like! I have to be strong! I can't afford to crack or the sadness might pour out and drown me! Don't tell me to let it all hang out! I've been holding it in too long.*

"This is how I am," I said. "The fleas go with the dog."

"Your grandmother again?"

"My friend Dave." I had to smile.

"The guy with the hog? Cute couple," Raymond said. "I just want you to know that you don't have to pretend with me."

"And you don't have to feel sorry for me, Raymond. Most of the time I like my life. That may sound crazy, but it's true. At the moment I'm just a little depressed because I thought Mother was coming back soon."

"What if she never comes back?" he asked.

My hand went to the little gold heart hidden in the hollow of my throat. I had faced this question a thousand times. There was only one answer.

"If she never comes back, I'll never know it," I

said, "because I'll always be waiting. I'll wait for Mother till the last minute."

His hands stroked my temples, my hair. I could imagine what he must be thinking. It has taken me these two years to accept the contradiction that Mother is as real as the breeze and as much of an illusion.

"I'm glad you told me, Livvy," he said. "We have to trust each other. We have to be close, no secrets between us."

"No secrets," I promised. My skin was burning. I wanted Raymond to leave so I could think about him.

He read my mind. "I have to run. Did I tell you I'm auditioning for the school play?"

"Word gets around."

"There are no secrets in Kumquat."

"Only a few," I said.

He grinned, skinning back his long black hair. "Liv, I hate to leave you in this big old haunted house."

"I've been haunting it for ages," I said. "I think I can make it through another afternoon." I opened the front door for Raymond. "Remember, you promised not to tell."

"Cross my heart. You keep my secret, too."

"Secrets are my specialty," I said.

He bent and kissed the top of my head, then streaked down the street like a beautiful animal.

I sat in the rocking chair in the parlor, retracing our conversation and the feel of his hands on my face. Then for a long time I looked in the mirror, trying to see who Raymond saw looking back at him.

11

Rosella could not understand why I had confided in Raymond.

"Well, I did."

"Why?"

"Because he's my friend."

We were standing in her front yard, by the naked forsythia bush. Running her fingers along a thin branch, she abruptly snapped it off.

"Aren't you rushing things? He's only been back for two months."

"I've known him since we were little kids."

"He's not a little kid anymore," she said.

I said, "It's perfectly natural for you to feel the way you do."

"What way is that?" Her body stiffened.

"Jealous," I whispered, avoiding her eyes.

"Jealous!" She gasped as if she'd been slapped. "Is that what you think I am?"

"Aren't you?"

"I don't know why I invited you for supper! I don't know why I did!" Rosella raged the length of the fence bordering the lawn and the bare oaks thrusting their black limbs into the sky. I had never seen her so angry.

"Are we having a real fight?" I asked. "If we are, I don't know how to act."

"If we are, you can thank your friend!" she snapped.

"All I said was—"

"I heard what you said! Jealous! That's a laugh!"

"I mean, you don't want to share me."

"Is that what he said?"

"No, I was just wondering."

"You make a lousy liar, Liv."

"Don't call me a liar."

"Don't act like one!"

"Look! I don't want to fight with you!"

"That makes two of us," she said.

"So let's stop."

"It's a little late for that."

"Okay, then let's pretend."

We sat in silence on the porch steps. The sky was colorless, promising nothing, as if it had forgotten what it meant to be the sky. It looked exactly the way I felt.

"I'm sorry I called you a liar, Liv."

"I'm sorry you were right."

"You were right too. I'm jealous," she admitted. "Lately, you spend so much time with him, and then when we're together, all we do is fight."

"That's not his fault."

"Whose fault is it?"

"Rosella, why won't you give him a chance? You

don't even know him and you've made up your mind."

"I know him," she said. "He's always talking about himself; impressing everybody with these big stories about the things he's done and the plays he's been in, and everybody eats it up, like we're the audience and he's a star shining down on us."

I knew what she meant; Raymond tends to show off, but sweetly, like a little child, who doesn't feel alive unless people are watching him.

"He's just different from people around here, that's all."

"He doesn't seem real," she insisted.

"He's real," I said, recalling his hands, his thumb lightly stroking my wrist.

She sighed. "I hope you're right. Did he promise not to tell?"

"Crossed his heart."

"Was he surprised to find out about your mother?"

"Rosella, you should've seen his face!"

We laughed. It felt so good to be allies again. In the empty days when Mother first left, it was the laughter we shared that saved me. The choice was simple: crack up laughing or crack up period. And we talked; we had left no subject undiscussed. It was Rosella's voice that had sustained me.

"Do you think you'll ever get married?" I asked her.

"Yes, I think so."

"I won't," I said.

"How do you know?"

"I don't know, I just do."

"You might meet someone you love," she said, "and want to be with him forever."

"Loving somebody doesn't mean you stay together."

"Sometimes it does," she said. "Look at my parents."

"They seem so happy. Do they ever fight?"

Rosella hooted. "Do they ever! You should've heard

them the other night, arguing about who lost the car keys: 'Well, I sure didn't.' 'Well, I sure didn't.' 'Well, I haven't driven that car since Christmas!' 'Well, I haven't driven that car since we bought it!' Boy, it was really ridiculous! Go ahead, laugh, they deserve it.''

"But then they make up," I said, "and everything's fine."

"Yes," Rosella said gently. "Everything's fine..."

Her mother opened the front door and said, "Supper's ready. You girls finished hollering?"

Rosella hauled me to my feet and we went inside.

I like her family. They kid around a lot. Her little brother Marc, who's eight, pretended to throw a bowl of mashed potatoes at me.

"Put that down, Marc. Liv, how's your mother?"

"Fine, Mr. Jensen. How are you?"

"Can't complain."

"He usually does," Marc said.

"Just eat," his father told him.

Mr. Jensen works at the quarry, like most of the men in town. Mrs. Jensen is a secretary at the school.

Rosella's big brother John was there, too. He's a deputy sheriff with the county. When our part-time police chief (and full-time plumber) has his hands full, John is sent to help him out.

"More roast beef, Liv?"

"It's so good, Mrs. Jensen!"

She beamed. "I know it's your favorite."

Rosella asked John about life in the big city.

"It's much too big-time for you, little sister."

"Big of you to drop by," she said.

"Man!" Marc exclaimed. "When *I* get out of Kumquat, I'm *never* coming back!"

"Never?" wondered his mother.

He reconsidered. "Well, I might come back on my

birthday and at Christmas, and maybe for Thanksgiving, too.''

"Where will you be the rest of the time?" I asked.

"Someplace making gold records. I'm gonna be a big rock star."

"You can't be a rock star," John said.

"Why not?"

"You sing too good. All those singers sound like this: Ooooh wah oh arrrggghhh—''

"Just wait till I'm famous." Marc pointed his fork at John. "All those newspaper reporters will ask me about my family. I'll say, 'Brother? What brother? I haven't got no brother.' ''

"*Any* brother," his mother corrected.

"See!" Marc crowed. "Mom agrees with me!"

For dessert, we had another of my favorites: warm apple pie with vanilla ice cream. Everyone lingered over coffee, talking. It would be lovely to be part of a family that loved each other; a family that liked each other, too. Last year they all went to Disneyland, and next summer they'll skin-dive off the Mexican coast.

I can recall only one family outing when all four of us were present. We went to the circus in Sacramento. Although unforgettable, it was not a joyous event. My father, never a falling-down drunk, had been higher than the aerial acts. The circus people depressed Grandmother. She said they had terrible teeth. Mother had been upset by the animals. She said the people had a choice, teeth or no teeth, but the animals were caged and couldn't leave. We were the only family rooting for the lions, not the trainer. "Weirdo!" Mother had shouted at the strapping blond man with his crackling whip and his spangled tights.

Then the day was capped by a three-hour drive in search of a fabulous Italian restaurant that my father insisted we must not miss. Unfortunately, we missed it.

After extensively touring the abandoned warehouse section of town, and every other section but the one containing the restaurant, we stumbled across a freeway entrance and inadvertently headed home.

It was not an occasion that I will describe to my grandchildren, should that day and phantom family ever come. Or maybe I will.

Mrs. Jensen gave me a large wedge of pie to take home.

"See that your mother gets some," she said, "and give her my best. It's funny we've never even met, you girls being such good friends all this time."

"I know she'd enjoy meeting you," I said, glad for a chance to tell her the truth.

John offered to walk me home but I declined. "It's just around the corner, and the moon is full. I'll be fine."

"Full moons bring out the weirdos," he insisted.

"Like him," Rosella finished.

We convinced John that Kumquat was free of werewolves, kidnappers and international terrorists.

Rosella came to the sidewalk with me. I knew she had something to say.

"I'm sorry about this afternoon. I blew it."

"Me too," I said.

"I don't care if you're friends with Raymond, as long as you're still friends with me."

"We'll always be friends," I promised. "Nothing will stop us. Neither snow, nor rain, nor Raymond Mooney—"

"That's the post office's motto."

"They've had trouble with him, too?"

Silly, but it made her smile.

"Well, goodnight."

"Goodnight." I hugged her quickly. Lack of practice made me awkward. She looked surprised and embarrassed and glad.

The moon followed me home. It filled the sky, paling all but the most determined stars. I remembered one of my last conversations with Mother. We had just finished a typically odd yet nourishing meal: baked bean sandwiches, cranberry sauce and green olives. We sat outside in the warm, still night, the porch swing creaking like crickets.

"Look, Mother! The Big Dipper."

"Where?"

"Right there, next to the big blue star; the one that looks like Grandmother's diamond."

"Oh, Livvy," Mother sighed. "I sure miss her. And I miss your father so much it hurts."

"He's been gone a long time," I said.

"The love doesn't change. It's still in my heart, and I keep waiting and waiting . . . I thought he would come back, if I waited long enough. Do you think I'll ever see him again?"

Waiting, hoping, Mother had held her breath; like a child leaning toward the birthday candles, making her wish.

Her answer lay beyond us in the sparkling darkness.

"I don't know, Mother," I said. "I hope so."

12

Dave was sitting on the bench outside the pharmacy, reading the latest *Messenger*, which I had just finished delivering. Jimmy Dean stood curbside, monitoring the traffic, his fat face almost smiling.

Dave's shoulders shook with raspy laughter. I sat down and scanned the editorial page, to see what was giving him fits.

Under the heading MORE BOOING THAN USUAL, was the following letter:

Editor:
As Mayor of Kumquat I was invited to participate in the town of Cedar's 63rd Annual Harvest Festival Parade. This is always a spectacular event, with balloons and Shriners and high school bands; exactly the kind of thing we'd like to see in Kumquat.

At any rate, I happily accepted the invitation, as I never pass up an opportunity to publicize our fair town. This I do at my own expense. I have never used a dime of the taxpayers' money.

In any event, I drove my completely restored, classic 1934 Packard LeBaron in the parade. I think you all know what that car means to me.

As I drove along the parade route, waving to the audience and throwing candy at children, I seemed to notice more booing than usual. This I attributed to the shocking decline in respect shown to those who hold public office. It's a difficult job and Mr. Lincoln said it best when he said you can please some of the people some of the time but the rest are complainers and not worth worrying about.

Be that as it may, there was a great deal of booing and some laughter and rude remarks, but I continued to smile and wave as though nothing were wrong.

Imagine my shock and disgust when I reached the fair grounds, parked my car, and discovered a bumper sticker taped to the back of my Packard: GIRLS WANTED. NO EXPERIENCE NECESSARY.

There's nothing funny about this! This disgraceful perversion must stop! The person(s) responsible for this reprehensible crime must be ferreted out and turned over to the proper authorities for disposal. This act was a blot not only on my bumper, but on the proud name of Kumquat as well.

If you have any information concerning the identity of the person(s) involved, please write to me or drop by my hardware store, open 8-5, Monday through Saturday, Sunday noon to four.

Stamp out crime before it stamps out you.

Cordially,

(Mayor) Bob Block

Block's Hardware, Kumquat

"I wish I knew that person's identity!" Dave chortled. "I'd shake his hand and take him out to dinner."

"You don't think it's a blot on the proud name of Kumquat?"

"If we can survive the mayor, we can survive anything! I feel like celebrating. Join me for some chow, sis. My treat."

We went into the Cough Up and took the front table, overlooking the street. It was warm and cozy and the windows were steamy. Jimmy Dean glared in at us, distinctly annoyed.

Betty set down our coffees so firmly they sloshed. "I don't care how cold he is, Dave. I'm not letting that hog in here."

"A hog in a restaurant? I should say not," Dave said.

"You know what happened the last time," she said. "The mayor came in and made a big fuss."

"He's always making a fuss," Dave said. "Did you see his letter in the paper? It's a pip."

"He says I shouldn't even let Jimmy stand outside," Betty mourned. "He says it's bad for business."

"Bad for business!" Dave was outraged. "That's the stupidest thing I've ever heard! Jimmy's like having a truck parked outside. Everybody knows truckers find the best restaurants! Everybody knows hogs love food!"

"There's nothing you can say, Dave; he's not coming in here. Jimmy's got thick skin. He's not cold. Is he?"

"Is he what?" Dave perused the menu, even though he knew it by heart.

"Cold," Betty said. "He looks so naked."

"That's how he's supposed to look. You can dress up a hog but he's still a pig."

"Well, tell him to stop staring at me! Oh, I can't stand that sad expression on his face."

Betty brought Jimmy a big bowl of coffee thick with cream and chopped crullers.

Dave had the minestrone soup and the veal cutlet. I had two green salads, mine and Dave's, and steak with golden gravy and a pile of mashed potatoes. For dessert we had chocolate pudding.

Satisfied, Dave pushed back from the table. "Get enough to eat, sis?"

I groaned.

"That's what I like to hear. You look a little skinny around the edges lately. Guess you're going through one of those growing spurts."

Dave's known me since I was a brand-new baby. He's seen my outside change and change. In the seventeen years I've known him, Dave's outside hasn't aged a day. He was born bald and stayed that way, he says. He's rugged as an old oak.

Inside Dave, that's another story, and one he seldom tells. He lost his wife ten years ago. They shared forty years of married life. When you live with and love somebody so long, they take part of you with them when they go.

There were never any children, and I was sorry about that, because Dave would have made a tremendous dad. His sheep and cattle ranch is way up in the hills. He lives alone, but for Jimmy Dean.

"Sometimes I sit and think," he sighed, contented. "Other times, I just sit."

Jimmy looked contented, too. He was snoozing on the sidewalk, snugly draped with tablecloths, looking like a mound of fresh snow.

"Dave, did you ever think of leaving Kumquat?"

"Leave?" He grinned and shook his head. "That'd be like leaving my skin."

"Sometimes I think about leaving."

"You mean for college?"

"No, just leaving," I said. I didn't want to go home to my empty house. I wanted to stay with Dave, where it was bright and warm and safe. To my horror, the bridge of my nose began to burn. I was going to cry.

"Are you okay, Liv?"

"Fine. Just tired."

"You look a little strange."

"I am a little strange."

"You sure you're not lonesome?"

I was instantly on the alert. "Why would I be lonesome?"

"Who isn't?" Dave said. "It's the nature of the beast. No matter how close you get to people, you're all alone in your skin, and you can't get out, and they can't get in, and it knocks you for a loop when you know it. For a loop..." Dave pocketed his waving hands. "It's kind of hard to put it into words."

"I know."

"Remember that song your daddy used to sing? I always liked that song. 'Kumquat may, I'll always love you; Kumquat may, I'll always care; Kumquat may, we'll—'"

"'—be together,'" I helped him. "'Someday, somewhere.'"

"'Kumquat may, I won't regret you; Kumquat may, I will be true; Kumquat may,'" Dave sang, "'I won't forget you, How could I forget a love like you?'... Wonderful song. The guys at Iffy's loved it. Your dad got a million requests for that song. He should've tried to get it on the radio."

"He did try."

"Oh well," Dave said.

A car honked as it drove by in the dusk. We raised our hands in greeting.

"You've always got me, sis," Dave said quickly.

"And Mother."

"Of course. How's your mother?"

"Just fine." I hate lying to Dave.

"I hear she's working over in Cedar. Funny how things turn out. I knew your dad when he was just a little boy. Now look at his baby, all grown up. Wouldn't he think you were something."

"I wish he wasn't dead." My hands flew to my mouth. I instantly regretted that I'd put Dave on the spot.

"Me too," he murmured. "You know it, sis." Then he kindly directed my attention to the street. "There goes the mayor. Yoo-hoo, Bobby! Loved your letter!" Dave waved frantically as the mayor drove by. Needless to say, he didn't wave back. He pointed a poisonous finger at Jimmy, who was on his feet, trailing table-cloths, looking like the ghost of a Frigidaire.

Dave bought me a couple of chocolate mints and helped himself to a toothpick. The night was cold. Jimmy was thrilled to see us; he galloped toward Dave's truck, which was parked around the corner. Dave started up the sidewalk, then stopped.

"Liv," he began, grabbing his nose, as though he didn't like what was coming next. "I got something to say, and there's no easy way, so I'm going to have to spit it out."

Inside, I screamed: *He knows about Mother!*

I kept my face as smooth as cream. "What is it, Dave?"

"Word is you're hanging around with Raymond Mooney."

Relief made me weak. I dropped to my knees and pressed my ear to the sidewalk.

"Yep," I said. "That's what I hear."

Dave scowled. "I know, it's none of my business, but Raymond Mooney—"

"We're just good friends! Why does everybody in this town have us married off?"

"I've known you both since you were kids," he said, "and that boy came back different. He's changed."

"Of course he's changed. He's all grown up!"

"That's not it," Dave insisted. "He's too flashy. He acts like he's on some TV show."

"Just because he doesn't wear overalls and a cowboy hat doesn't make him a Communist," I said. "He's been living in Los Angeles. Things are different there."

"No kidding." Dave thinks of southern California as a foreign country.

I wished I could explain Raymond so Dave and Rosella would understand him. If they knew his secrets, they would see below the surface. All they see now is an alien.

"Dave, there's nothing to worry about. Raymond and I are friends, that's all."

He stared at his boots. "I don't mean to butt in."

"You're not."

"Yes, I am. My problem is, I still see you as a little girl. But you take good care of yourself, don't you, Liv."

"I try."

"I know you do."

The lights from Loretta's Deli silvered his bristly cheeks. A childhood chant zinged through my brain. *Reverso Shaving Cream! Buy Some Today! Reverso! Makes your whiskers grow inside and you bite 'em off!*

"Well, goodnight, Liv."

"Thanks for supper."

"My pleasure." His heels rang down the sidewalk.

I climbed into the Plymouth and drove the few blocks

home. The mailbox was damp and bare. The house seemed as hugely hollow as a castle on the moor. Moors are endless, rolling wastelands, where people in novels wander when they go crazy.

When I fell alseep I dreamed I was awake. The Plymouth wouldn't start. The engine was dead. Mrs. Wallis floated by in a slinky red dress. *That's not like you*, I said. *I know,* she gushed. *Isn't it wonderful?*

A silvery image pressed into my mind: a spoon, bending under Raymond's caress. *Look, Olivia! Magic!* he whispered. *Plastic,* Rosella sighed, turning her face away.

Downtown. No one around but Jimmy Dean. The sidewalks and streets were deserted. Jimmy had a suitcase; he was trying to hitch a ride. I begged him not to leave but he was determined. He said: *Things aren't always the way they seem*. I said: *Pigs don't talk*. He shrugged. *People don't listen*.

I was in my bed. I was listening to the wind. No, it was a woman's voice; a beautiful woman speaking music.

She covered me like a willow tree, her long hair falling like summer rain. She was going to tell me the secret of life.

Olivia, she said, and her voice was my breath; her voice was all I would ever need. *Always remember, and never forget—*

The alarm clock buzzed and I woke up weeping.

Always remember what? Don't leave me.

13

The grocery bag split as hit the counter, sending onions bouncing on the kitchen floor, but I grabbed the phone before it stopped ringing. Raymond was supposed to call.

"Hello?"

"Luna Lee, is that you?"

I sank to the linoleum, stricken. It was Uncle Sargent's wife, my Aunt Cecilia.

"Are you there, Luna Lee?"

"It's me, Aunt Cece. It's Liv."

"You sound just like your mother. Why are you panting?" Her tart voice chilled my ear.

"I was running for the phone. How are you?"

"The point is, how are *you*? We never hear a word. Is your mother there? And don't tell me she's in the shower again. I swear, she must have a phobia."

A vision of Aunt Cece's shrewd, narrow face appeared on my kitchen ceiling. The ceiling was gauzy with gray cobwebs. The walls were dingy. The floor was sticky. What was the point? Why bother living?

My aunt is like a shot of a powerful depressant. I could feel her entering my veins.

"Mother's not in the shower; she's at work."

That slowed her down some. "Work? You mean in a store, or door to door?"

"Not exactly," I said. "She goes to parties and demonstrates stuff and people buy it."

Aunt Cece was half on and half off the phone. "Parties," she was telling Uncle Sargent. "Luna Lee goes to parties and demonstrates. That's her job."

My uncle commandeered the phone.

"Olivia, this is your Uncle Sargent. What's this about your mother going to parties?"

"She sells cosmetics," I said. "It's like Tupperware parties without the Tupperware."

"Put her on. I want to talk to her."

"She's not here right now."

"You're all alone?"

No, there's a biker gang in the bedroom.

"It's okay, Uncle Sargent. I'm seventeen."

"I don't care if you're forty-two. That's no reason for your mother to run around. Does she need the money?"

"We're doing fine. She wanted something to do in her spare time."

"She could stay home and take care of you," her brother said.

There are worse things than being an only child.

"I'm calling about Thanksgiving," he said.

"Thanksgiving?" I echoed faintly.

"Can you hear me, Liv? Is this another bad connection?"

Our conversations are frequently cut short by "bad connections."

Me: "Uncle Sargent? Are you there? I can't hear you!"

Him: "Stop shouting. I can hear you just fine."

Me: "There's too much static on the line. Hello? Hello?"

Him: "Put your mother on the phone!"

Me: "I can't hear you so I'm hanging up . . ."

Or sometimes the line goes dead.

"We're all getting together for Thanksgiving," my uncle said. "I won't accept any excuses this time."

Why do they want to spend the day with us? We drive them crazy. They think we're nuts. They criticize us from the moment they arrive until their car backs out of the driveway.

"Maybe. I don't know," I said.

"It's settled. You've missed the last two years."

"I wish we could come, but our car isn't running."

"We're coming to you."

My mind split open and my brains ran out. In desperation I blurted, "Mother might have to work."

"On Thanksgiving?"

"Lots of people are home that day."

"That's ridiculous," he said.

"I know." The conversation was skidding out of control. I didn't know how to get rid of him. Maybe Mother could convince him. I had no choice. "Oh, here's Mother now. She's just coming in. Hold on, please."

I set down the receiver, tiptoed across the room, slammed the back door and picked up the phone.

"Sargent," I said in Mother's voice. "How nice of you to call!"

"Luna Lee?" he growled. "I can't believe it's you. We were beginning to think you were dead."

"No such luck." I laughed Mother's laugh. "I'm just pretty busy these days."

"Every time we call you're in the shower. Doesn't Liv ever give you the message?"

"Nobody's home when I call back," I said. "Did she tell you about my job?"

"Something about parties or going to demonstrations—"

"I do a lot of traveling," I said. "I'll tell you about it sometime."

"We're coming for Thanksgiving," he announced.

"I'm working," I shot back.

"Nobody works on Thanksgiving!"

"I know. That's why it's one of our biggest days." I could hear the steam hissing from my uncle's ears. "Look!" he barked. "What's more important: money or your family?"

"Speaking of families, how are Mom and Dad?"

"Fine, as if you care."

"Won't they be joining you for the holiday?"

After a pause he stiffly admitted, "They're spending it in Las Vegas."

"I hear it's lovely this time of year."

"Don't be a smartypants!" he hollered. He's used to running over Mother like a steamroller. This time she wasn't playing dead.

"Sargent, I'd love to chat, but I have an appointment. Can I call you back?"

"Don't you dare hang up! You never call back! Besides, there's nothing further to discuss. We're coming for Thanksgiving and that's final."

"What did you say? Can you hear me, Sargent?"

"Don't give me that baloney! I hear you fine! We'll be there on Thursday and so will you!"

"What? The connection must be going bad."

"Thursday!" he screamed. "We're bringing the bird!"
And he slammed down the phone.

14

On Wednesday Raymond helped me with my Thanksgiving preparations. Rosella planned to come but she changed her mind when she found out Raymond would be there.

I wasn't sorry she stayed home. All they do is bicker; picking and poking at each other like children. There would be plenty of that when my relatives arrived. Besides, it was fun having Raymond to myself. The work melted away with his help.

We split wood, washed windows, scrubbed floors and polished silver. He mowed the lawn and trimmed the hedge while I dusted the parlor, sparing Mama Spider's web, and watched him from the window.

His faded jeans were the color of the sky. His black hair slashed across his forehead and his cheeks were very red. For a moment I pretended we were a young married couple. Raymond caught me watching him and smiled.

We peeled turnips and potatoes, slathered cream cheese on celery and baked two pumpkin pies. The kitchen was steamy and rich with the smell of cinnamon and allspice.

Raymond asked if I'd heard from Mother.

"No, I didn't think I would."

A lie. As Thanksgiving drew near, I had hoped she was closer and that at any moment the door would burst open—

"Liv." Raymond gently tugged my braid. "You have to face the fact that you'll probably never see her again."

"I will." I moved away from him, angry.

"You don't even know where she is."

"So? She says she's coming back in her letters."

"But she doesn't show up," he said.

"I know Mother, and I know she'll be back, even though I don't know when. Now please, let's talk about something else. I've got enough on my mind already."

"I'm sorry," he said. "Don't be mad, Livvy."

"I'm not mad."

"Yes, you are."

"Will you please stop telling me I'm mad when I'm not?"

"Then why are you making that face?"

"What face?"

"This one."

His imitation made me laugh. "I don't look like that!"

"No, you look pretty good now," he said, kissing the tip of my nose. We talked and worked until his mother phoned up and invited him home.

*   *   *

"It's freezing!" Uncle Sargent bellowed, climbing out of the car, scowling at me as if I were responsible for the weather.

I watched from the porch as the Ford disgorged them. Thirteen-year-old Sargent Jr. (known as Sandy) and eleven-year-old Ronny tumbled out of the backseat in a wrestling hold. Wendy, who's my age, wrinkled her nose as if she smelled something bad. Aunt Cece whisked a scarf off her tower of frozen yellow waves and frowned at me.

"Olivia, where's your mother?"

"Come on in!" I beat a hasty retreat inside the house. If there was going to be a scene, which was guaranteed, I wanted it conducted in private.

There was more than a scene; we staged an opera.

"What do you mean, your mother's not here?" my uncle bawled, turning purple.

"She told you she'd probably have to work," I said.

"You mean we drove all this way for nothing?" Wendy whined.

"There's a limit," Aunt Cece told Uncle Sargent. "I don't know why you put up with it."

"Mother said she'd call later. She said she was sorry but this was an emergency."

"A cosmetics emergency?" My uncle's cheeks quivered. "What is the name of this company she works for?"

"Mystery Woman Cosmetics," I said. "You've probably seen their ad on TV: 'Your eyes will be the guise with which you weave a web of—'"

"Gees!" Ronny shouted. "Look at this spiderweb!"

"Don't touch it!" I yelped. "It's for school," I added. "We're studying arachnids."

"How do you turn this thing on?" Sandy asked, pulling a knob off the TV set.

My uncle, a big man, was immense with indignation. "Just wait until the folks hear about this! You try to have a little family feeling—we went and bought that beautiful bird!"

"Don't get yourself worked up," my aunt said. "That's just the kind of person she is. Don't let it bother you. Try to stay calm. What on *earth* is *wrong* with that woman?"

"There's nothing wrong with Mother," I said.

"Oh brother," Wendy snickered.

"Are we going home now?" Sandy said.

"No, we're not going home!" said his father. "We're here, and we're going to have a family Thanksgiving, with or without Luna Lee!"

Aunt Cece rolled her eyes and reluctantly removed her coat. "Get the stuff out of the car," she told the boys.

"He'll go, he'll go!" they chorused, batting each other. They were flopped in front of the TV set, watching a football game.

"Did you hear your mother? Get the damn bird! *Run, you sonuvaguns!*" their father hollered. The boys leaped up and shot out the door. "You like football, Liv?"

"Not really."

"Why not?"

"I don't know. It's so violent, I guess."

"It's only a game," Wendy said.

We watched a bone-crunching pile-up. The crowd cheered as the injured players were carried off the field.

"It seems like a lot of people get hurt."

"People get hurt every day," Wendy said. "What about car accidents? Do you want to make cars illegal? People choke to death on bananas, you know."

"Wendy's a cheerleader for the Trojans," said Aunt Cece. "You should see her outfit. It's adorable. I'll put this turkey in the oven to keep it warm...Olivia, what's this mess?"

"Mess?"

Aunt Cece had her head in the oven. "It looks like sweet potatoes."

I sighed. "I forgot to take them out."

"It doesn't matter. Nobody in our family likes sweet potatoes."

"Especially when they've exploded," Wendy said.

"I'll scrape them out later."

"Right," Wendy said. "Don't do it now. You'll ruin your pretty dress."

My only real dress was several years old; too tight under the arms and out of fashion. I realized I looked like a refugee, not dolled-up as I'd imagined.

The table was already set, gleaming with linen and silver and the delicate flowered china Grandmother gave my parents when they married. There was little left to do and even less to say. We watched the football game while the vegetables cooked. Wendy thumbed through Mother's latest issue of *Redbook*.

"I can't understand why your mother lets you keep that spider," Aunt Cece said.

"She's hiding now, but she's pretty," I said.

"Your mother?" Wendy tittered.

"The spider."

"How do you know she's a she?" my uncle said.

"One time she had babies. I carried them out to the garden."

"Your grandmother, too," Aunt Cece said. "She was always a little eccentric."

"You wouldn't dare say that if she were still alive."

"Of course not." Aunt Cece snorted. "That would be rude."

"How soon are we going to eat?" asked her husband.

"As soon as the vegetables are done. Olivia?"

I filled the serving bowls and set them on the table, which had been turned so the family could watch TV. Uncle Sargent sat at the head of the table. I sat between Wendy and Aunt Cece. The only way to survive this day was to pretend it was a memory. Only a dream.

Aunt Cece was saying something to me. "I expect we'll see your mother then."

"When?" I was lost.

"When Grampa kicks off." Ronny grabbed a drumstick.

"Don't talk about your grandfather like that!" warned his father.

"She started it!"

"Don't call your mother 'she'!"

"What am I supposed to call her?"

"Don't talk fresh!"

Wendy eyed the table incredulously. "Mother, you know I only like jellied cranberry sauce! All she's got are those awful whole berries!"

"Put down that fork," Aunt Cece told Sandy. "We're going to say grace first."

"Grace first," he said, popping the stuffing into his mouth.

"Don't you dare swallow that!" thundered my uncle. "Olivia, give the blessing."

I looked around the table at my family. My family! Uncle Sargent, his hands clenched, his eyes squinched shut; Aunt Cece, bowing her Ferris wheel hair; Cousin Ronny, easing his thumb up his nose; Cousin Sandy, shifting the stuffing from cheek to cheek; Cousin Wendy, one hard eye peeled, nipping off blonde split ends with her long fingernails . . .

"Good Lord!" I croaked, unintentionally. Everyone jumped, then glared. "Oh Lord, let us be thankful for the food on this table and for all our many blessings, today and every day. Amen."

"And let us not forget, O Lord," continued Aunt Cece, "to thank Thee for bringing us together again. Most of us, that is, O Lord, though some of us apparently have better things to do—"

"Drop it, Amen," my uncle concluded. Sandy noisily swallowed the stuffing and proceeded to gulp more food. Bowls and platters spun around the table.

"I don't see why you're getting mad at her," Wendy said.

"At who?" Uncle Sargent was genuinely puzzled.

"At Mother, your wife, just because she said we wouldn't see Aunt Luna until Grampa's funeral. You know it's true."

"The subject is closed."

"Well, excuse me for living! You bad-mouth Luna Lee all the time, but if one of us says one little thing—"

"Shut up!" her father roared.

As if he had pressed an ejector button, Wendy shot up from the table, sobbing, and rocketed into the bathroom. One Christmas she locked herself in there and ate a whole pineapple that Grandmother had received from an old beau and planned to share with the family. It made her teeth so sensitive she couldn't eat for days.

"She's always locking herself in the can," Ronny said.

"Who cares?" Sandy crowed. "Now I can eat all her skin!"

Meaning the crisp turkey skin she'd piled on her plate.

"No, you cannot!" Wendy screamed through the door. "Mother, don't you dare let him have one shred!"

"Get out here right now!" her father yelled.

Ronny turned up the volume on the TV set.

Wendy finally flounced out of the bathroom, radiating Mother's favorite perfume. She was also wearing Mother's new lipstick.

Although I had barely touched my food, I doubted that I would ever eat again. This was no dream; it was hideously real. I was marooned with a mob of relative strangers, hunched around a big dead bird; its skin shorn, its leg bones bared, its thick flesh clogging my throat—

"What's wrong, Liv?" Aunt Cece was watching me.

"Nothing. I guess I'm not hungry."

"I'll eat your skin if you don't want it," Sandy said.

"Why are you looking at the turkey like that?" my uncle said. "You've got the strangest expression on your face."

"You're not going to puke, are you?" Wendy demanded, moving her chair a safe distance away.

"No, I'm fine." My head felt light. I tried to laugh. "I think I just became a vegetarian."

"That figures," Wendy said.

"What's that?" Ronny asked.

"Someone who won't eat meat," said his father.

"Why not?"

"Because they think it's mean to the poor old bird."

"I'm not usually like this," I explained. "I just happened to notice that the turkey's dead."

"Be hard to eat if it wasn't," Sandy said. "It'd be flying all over the table!"

This produced much merriment until Wendy pointed out that turkeys don't fly.

"Not when they're dead!" Uncle Sargent crossed his eyes and got the giggling going again.

"I thought you loved turkey, Liv." Aunt Cece looked tragic.

"I do. It's just— Everything tastes great. Excuse me." I headed for the bathroom.

Locking the door behind me, I started the cold water rushing in the sink, then sank down on the edge of the tub, my face pressed to the porcelain. I sat there for a long time.

There was a knock at the door. "Are you all right, Liv?"

"Yes, Aunt Cece."

"Other people have to use the bathroom, too. I can go upstairs."

"No, I'm coming out right now."

Uncle Sargent was telling an ethnic joke. I contemplated a return engagement in the bathroom.

"Pass the gravy," Aunt Cece said.

I nibbled a celery stalk while she described Wendy's enormous popularity: Boys kept calling her all the time, the phone was forever ringing. They were thinking of getting Wendy her own number and Princess phone; it was the only way they could squeeze in a call.

"Do you have a boyfriend, Liv?"

Aunt Cece prattles on while your mind floats away, then she reels you back with a zap.

"I have friends who are boys."

"Lucky you," Wendy said. "I got eight invitations to the Thanksgiving dance."

"We don't have a Thanksgiving dance," I said, "but at Halloween—"

"I am getting so fat!" Wendy moaned.

"Honey, no, you're not," protested her mother.

"I am so! Look at my stomach!"

"You're right, it's kind of fat," Sandy said.

"Look who's talking, buffalo belly!"

"Barge bottom!"

"Bubble butt!"

I excused myself to dish up the dessert.

Wendy examined a spoonful of pumpkin pie and topping. "Is this Cool Whip?"

"No, it's real cream."

"Too bad. I like Cool Whip better."

The family shared this sentiment. Nevertheless, each member managed to wolf down several slabs. Uncle Sargent regaled us with his prehistoric views on life. The football game blared in the background.

More than ever before, I knew how Mother must have felt, struggling to grow up under her family's crushing thumbs. How she must have dreamed of her escape! When she married my father and her parents disowned her, she thought she was finally safe. But no; Uncle Sargent wouldn't let her go. He and his wife and their rabid brats invaded her home again and again, until it didn't feel like her home anymore. They were never really her family. She was nothing to them. They were nothing to me.

The phone rang and I ran for it.

"Let me talk to her," my uncle said.

Rosella's voice was as warm as pie. "You still have the strength to answer the phone. That's a good sign. How's it going?"

Laughter hatched deep inside me. "The way you'd expect."

"That bad, huh?"

"I wouldn't say that."

"They're listening, right?"

"That's right, Mother. Uncle Sargent is standing by."

"You poor thing. You'll be rewarded in heaven."

"Promise?"

"Liv, are you sure this will work?"

"Positive. They're dying to talk to you."

"They sound like complete creeps."

"Absolutely. Here comes Uncle Sargent now."

"Talk to you later."

"Sure, we'll hold." I handed the phone to Uncle Sargent. "Mother will be right back. She had to answer the door."

"Where is she?"

"The Holiday Inn in Fresno."

There's probably a Holiday Inn in Fresno. There's probably one on Mars.

"Excuse me," I told my aunt and cousins as I hurried through the dining room into the john.

Ronny said, "She's probably puking her guts up again."

"Quit talking about puke! You're making me sick!" Wendy shrieked.

I locked the bathroom door and turned on the faucets, full blast. Then I slipped through the other door, the one leading to the little room where Mother slept after my father died.

I wanted to climb into the bed and pull the quilt over my head, but I plopped her autograph hound in my lap and picked up the extension. On her end, Rosella silently hung up. It worked exactly as we'd planned. No muss, no fuss, no telltale dial tone.

"Hello, Sargent. Happy turkey day!" I said, fingering the gold heart at my throat.

"Luna Lee, where on earth are you? Liv said something about the Holiday Inn—"

"We're having a sales convention."

"On Thanksgiving Day? That doesn't make sense. If I didn't know better, I'd think you'd arranged this trip on purpose, to avoid being with your family. You haven't even asked about Mom and Dad."

"How are they?"

"Terrible. They postponed their trip. Dad's been having some problems with his heart."

"I didn't know he had one." I couldn't resist.

"What?"

"You heard me."

My uncle exploded. "You don't know a damn thing about hearts, except how to break them! You know what you did! You broke their hearts when you married that man!"

"Sargent, I didn't call to start a fight. I called to wish you a happy Thanksgiving."

"Too bad you're not here to do it in person."

"You know how it is when you have a job."

"A job is more important than your family?"

"A job helps support my daughter," I said.

"And you think it's right to leave her alone on Thanksgiving?"

"She's not alone. She's in the bosom of her loving family."

"Sarcasm is not one of your strong suits, Luna Lee."

"What makes you think I'm being sarcastic? Don't you love Olivia?"

"You know what your problem is, Luna Lee? Your problem is you've always done exactly what you wanted, without thinking of anybody else!"

I was hot. "That's not true! You always told me what to do! You and the folks were on me every second!"

"Because you were too scatterbrained to look after yourself! That was evident in every action you took!"

"I didn't take any action! You wouldn't let me! Every time I tried to stand on my own two feet, you reached down and pulled the rug right out from under me! Why Mom and Dad egged you on I'll never know."

"You disappointed them!"

"They disappointed me!"

"Your daughter is a goddamned vegetarian!" boomed my uncle. "And God knows what else! Imagine what she gets into while you're running all over the countryside, going to conventions and parties!"

This was too much. I rushed to my own defense.

"Liv is a wonderful girl," I said, "more responsible and capable and independent than your three idiot children can ever hope to be!"

My uncle was shocked to his shoes. "Are you drunk? You've been drinking, haven't you."

"No, I feel fine. For the first time in my life I'm speaking my mind."

I could hear my uncle's lid rattle. He was coming to a full boil.

"I believe you've gone completely around the bend this time, Luna Lee. That's the only possible explanation. I'm going to hang up now and I don't expect to hear from you until you're ready to apologize. Is that clear?"

"Sargent?"

"Yes?"

"Don't hold your breath."

"I'm hanging up right now!" he howled.

"Me first!" I beat him to it.

I closed the door to Mother's bedroom and flushed the toilet, then went back into the dining room, where a storm of activity was taking place. Uncle Sargent was snatching up their belongings and thrusting them into grocery bags.

"What did Mother have to say?"

He shot me a look that would have brought a charging rhino to its knees.

"Your mother—Your mother!" Words failed him. His bulging eyeballs rolled up into his head.

"Those are Liv's crackers," Aunt Cece said, wrestling the Ritz box from his rigid fingers. "We certainly don't want to take anything that isn't ours."

Uncle Sargent began again. "Your mother is the most rude—the most rude, selfish, inconsiderate—"

"—immature," prompted my aunt.

"—immature woman I have ever met! And I've met them all, in the insurance business! She needs psychiatric help!"

"Mother's not crazy."

"Face facts." Wendy sneered.

"How would you like to eat a Princess phone?"

"Olivia!" warned Aunt Cece.

"I'm not going to stand here and let her insult Mother!"

"Coats!" bellowed Uncle Sargent. "Coats! Get your coats!"

"We'll miss the end of the game!" Sandy whined.

"Get your coat on and get in the car!"

"Wait a minute! They're kicking off!"

"*I'll kick you over the fence!*" vowed his father.

"It's not my fault Aunt Luna's crazy!" Sandy skulked out the door.

Aunt Cece stuffed the turkey carcass into a bag and scooped up the after-dinner mints she'd placed on the coffee table. Ronny crammed handfuls of Ritz crackers into his pockets.

I watched from the porch as they poured into the Ford. My uncle stuck his big red face out the window.

"You tell your mother we won't be back! You tell her I expect an apology!"

My neighbor, Mrs. Harris, walking by with her beagle, politely pretended to be deaf. The news would be all over town that afternoon: LUNA LEE AND BROTHER BRAWL.

"Tell your mother I'll be waiting for her call!"

"Don't hold your breath," I said, as the car screeched down the street, sporting its new QUESTION AUTHORITY bumper sticker.

The house was mine again. It was a pleasure to clear the table, to wash the dishes in warm, silky suds; to wipe away all traces of the invasion.

Mother would be pleased. Uncle Sargent and Aunt Cece would no longer be a problem. There was a strong possibility we would never see them again, although Uncle Sargent would call repeatedly, to insist that we wouldn't be hearing from him.

I had burned the last bridge to Mother's family and was more alone than I had ever been.

It is a powerful feeling to know that you can do whatever you want. You can eat chocolate pudding for supper. You can stay up all night and watch TV. You can play the radio as loud as you like and toss dirty clothes on the floor.

You can dance down the stairs and spin like a top, till your long hair flies and your eyes are wild and nobody puts out a hand to stop you—

It is a powerful feeling to be on your own and to realize that the people you loved best are gone and to know that you can't penetrate the past and reclaim everything you've lost.

You have to move on, and you do your best, but sometimes you wonder if you'll always be alone, with no one beside you to admire the sunset, its golden yolk melting on a bed of pink clouds, the pink so precious that, if you had a dress that color, you'd be queen of the world, and you'd dance every dance.

Grandmother thought it was sinful to feel sorry for yourself. She thought it was sinful to feel sinful. She said we weren't put on the earth to suffer; we were here to keep our socks pulled up and to grab a laugh when we could.

I know I shouldn't complain but I wish—

Grandmother said if wishes were horses the streets would be full of manure.

I ate my supper in the kitchen. The rain began to fall, so strong and steady it seemed as if it had always been raining; as if it would rain forever.

The book I tried to read wouldn't keep me. I watched a rerun of *The Waltons*. I like those early episodes, before the mother left.

The stillness of the house overwhelmed me. I found myself hoping that the telephone would ring, longing for someone's warm voice in my ear; someone who would make me feel cozy and safe.

I thought I was going to call Rosella. But I didn't. I phoned Raymond.

15

December 2 (or 3, I think)
Santa Rosa, California
Dearest Liv,
How ARE you? Did you have a HAPPY THANKSGIV-
ING? I phoned that day but the line was busy. Did you
hear from Sargent & Cece?

I have gotten bogged down with a temporary job. As
you see, I'm learning to TYPE! This should come in
handy when I get home, because I'm thinking of writing
a romance novel! Why not? I've got the background for it!

Santa Rosa is a nice place. And I've discovered
something interesting! You know how lots of California
towns have Spanish names? Well, "San" comes before
towns with men's names: San Francisco (Francis), San
Bernardino (Bernard), San Jose (Jose), etc., and "Santa"

comes before women's names: Santa Barbara, Santa Monica, Santa Rosa, etc.

The only exception I've come across is "Santa Claus," but I think that's German, and anyway, it's not the name of a town.

Oh, well!

I hope you're happy and I'll see you soon. I love you, Liv. It's really true! Remember that song your father used to sing? That's how I feel about you!

Mother

XXXXXXXXXXXXXXXXXXXXXXXXXXXXXXXXXXXXXXXXX
OOOOOOOOOOOOOOOOOOOOOOOOOOOOOOOOOOOOOOOOOO

16

Change can be like grass growing; so gradual that you don't even notice till you're up to your knees in lawn.

Raymond is in my life now, blooming up through my

days, filling all the empty spaces. How could it ever
have been different?

Mornings, he's at my door to walk me to school.
Lunchtime, he waits for me out on the lawn or saves a
seat for me in the cafeteria when it's raining.

Afternoons, we walk home together, if he doesn't
have a rehearsal for the play or a basketball game. I feel
proud to sit in the stands and watch him score and hear
the crowd chant his name.

Raymond won the part of George in *Of Mice and
Men*. After valiantly resisting the director, Miss Maxwell, Bunky Block has been pressed into service as Lenny.

Nights, except when Rosella comes by, we study at
my kitchen table. Often, we end up talking. Mostly
Raymond talks and I listen, which is fine; he has so
many interesting things to say.

I like to hear about the places he's been and the
places he wants to go. Sometimes he even talks about
Holly. He showed me her photograph. She was as
beautiful as he'd said.

The kids at school think we're going together. I guess
that's so, though I'm not sure what it means. Merry
tells me how lucky I am. If she had her wish, she'd be me.

I only wish that having Raymond back in town hadn't
changed things between me and Rosella.

We don't see each other much, and when we do, we
try too hard and the words come out wrong, like
watching the keys when you type. The strain shows and
it's just not right; it used to be so easy for Rosella and me.

She never wants to be around Raymond, and if she
can't avoid it, she's silent. But I know what her eyes
say and it's not true. I did not go away from Rosella.
She went away from me.

I don't want to drift apart. I want to be friends, but
we can't seem to stop what has started. The more we

talk, the more we argue. She eats lunch with Merry and Kate and the girls. She's busy with school and in the afternoon she shelves books at the library. She breezes by me in the halls with this big smile: gee whiz, she'd love to talk but she's *so* busy...Raymond acts perfectly nice to her.

I miss her so much and I want to be close. I want to grab her and shake her and say: *Please! Let's stop it! I love you! Don't change!* But words don't work. We drift farther apart from each other, more distant than strangers.

Raymond had a rehearsal after school and I had to deliver the papers. I started home to get my car, wondering when the town's official Christmas decorations would come down. Big plastic candy canes flanked the main drag.

"Liv, wait up!"

Rosella overtook me, her bangs bobbing, slightly breathless.

"Feel like company?"

"Sure," I said. In the old days she never would have asked.

"Where's Raymond?" she said carefully.

"Rehearsing."

"He's a good actor."

I studied her to see what she meant. Her face was smooth and impassive.

"Miss Maxwell says he's very talented."

"She's right," Rosella said. We clomped along in silence. Before, there were not enough hours in the day for all we had to say to each other.

"How have you been?"

"Fine," she said. "And you?"

"Fine."

"Did you hear from your mother over Christmas?"

"Nope." After a pause, "I thought I would."

"That must've been disappointing," she said gently,

and I wanted to grab her hand and cry: *I thought she would come! I thought she was my present! Haven't I been good? Is Mother as real as Santa Claus? Why do I keep waiting?*

"Not really," I replied. "I'm used to it. Anyway, Raymond says she's probably gone forever."

"What does he know?"

"It's been more than two years."

"She writes you letters. She says she's coming back."

"But she never gets here, haven't you noticed? Mother was strange, but this is weird even for her. Raymond says I have to face reality."

"Who cares what Raymond says?" Rosella exclaimed. "It's not his life, it's yours!"

"I wish you wouldn't talk about him like that. It isn't nice to cast judgment."

The shock on her face was almost comical. "What about him, that first day we met? You think I don't know what he said about me?"

"He just didn't know you. I want him to know you. I want us all to be friends."

"You're incredible, Liv." She shook her head. "Don't you understand how things have changed? Everything's different."

"Nothing's different. The only difference is that Raymond is around sometimes."

"Sometimes! You never have a minute to yourself!"

"I'm by myself all the time, Rosella. I happen to enjoy his company, that's all."

"You used to enjoy my company, too."

"I do, but I'm tired of fighting."

"Me too."

We were standing in front of the library. Rosella waved to Mrs. Wallis, signaling that she was coming inside.

I took a deep breath and began again. "Did you have a good Christmas?"

"Yes," she said. "We went to my uncle's. I tried to phone you."

"I must've been at the Mooneys'," I said. "Raymond told them that Mother had been called out of town. They didn't want me to spend the day alone."

"How thoughtful."

"You don't need to act snotty!"

"Well, what could I do: tell my folks we couldn't go away because you were all alone? They think your mom's over there baking cocoa-cream clusters! That's the way you wanted it."

"I don't expect you to stay home."

"You act like Raymond cares about you and I don't!"

"Isn't it okay if he cares about me too? I can use all the care I can get!" I shouted. "You forget what it's like to be me, Rosella. You've got a great big huggy family. I've got no one! Ever tried to give yourself a hug? Months go by and nobody even touches me! Not my face or my hand or my arm. Not once! Did you know babies die if they're not cuddled? It's true! They've done studies!"

"So Raymond touches you?"

I almost slapped her face. "Not the way you're saying it! He makes me feel not so alone. He makes me feel like a girl."

"What the hell is that supposed to mean?"

I was stunned. Rosella never swears.

"You don't have to put your brains on ice. The other day he was changing the lightbulb over the kitchen sink!"

"So?"

"Since when have you forgotten how to change lightbulbs?"

"He's taller than me, Rosella. What's wrong with friends helping each other?"

"Nothing! But you're turning into the incredible shrinking woman! You can't even see what's in front of your face!"

"You're the only one who doesn't like him. Everybody thinks he's great."

"They're wrong! Don't you ever wonder about those stories he tells? How come we never saw those commercials he supposedly made?"

"Because they weren't shown in this area, that's why! That happens all the time with commercials."

"Oh, really?" Her lower lip curled. "I didn't know you were such an expert on the subject."

That steamed me. "Boy, you're acting like a jerk. You don't have to be so jealous of him."

"Jealous!"

"There's no reason why we can't still be friends."

"He's the reason!"

"There's things about Raymond you don't know," I said. "You'd feel differently if you knew the whole story."

"So tell me."

"I can't. I promised I wouldn't."

"We've never had secrets," she said.

"This has nothing to do with us! It's between Raymond and me."

Her chin trembled and her eyes burned with hurt, then her face closed tight, shutting me out.

"I don't know you anymore," she said. "Nothing you say or do makes sense."

"Thanks for the vote of confidence. Like you said, Rosella, it's my life."

She closed the library door between us. I watched her walk away, thinking of the things I wished I'd said, the snappy retorts I could have made, the explanations that would have proven her wrong. I was sick of her attacks on Raymond. I had never suspected that Rosella was so small. You never really know anyone, I thought.

When I stopped walking, I wasn't near home; I was in front of Iffy Murray's. Jimmy Dean stretched across the sidewalk, snoozing. "You big old pig," I whispered, scratching his belly. He opened one eye and grunted.

Inside, it was dark as a closet. My eyes adjusted and I located Dave, sitting at the bar with his cronies. "Sis!" he called, patting the empty stool beside him. Iffy Murray nodded hello as he solemnly polished a glass.

"Want a soda?" Dave asked. "A soda," he told Iffy, "and go easy on the ice."

Iffy squirted something brown and bubbly into a tumbler and set a bowl of unsalted peanuts by my elbow.

The place looked as though not a day had passed since I'd seen it last, years before. Watches ticked on the wall. Iffy's pedigreed boxer smiled doggedly from his gilt frame. Even Iffy looked unchanged, big and mild and white, as if he were carved from wax.

Any second my father might step out of the men's room, his rosy face smiling, his eyes shining, his hair combed smooth as glass.

Dave said, "How's it going?"

"Not too good."

He studied me, then picked up his glass, indicating a table with a jerk of his head. Iffy gave me a quarter for the jukebox. I punched up Teresa Brewer, his favorite.

"What's the problem?" Dave said. "Something happen at school?"

I shook my head no. "It's Rosella."

Her name burst from my throat like a sob. I pressed on, pretending not to notice. "We had a fight."

"About what?"

I hated to tell him. I knew exactly what Dave would say.

"Raymond Mooney. See, she says—"

"I knew it!" He thumped the table, making the vase of plastic flowers jump. "I knew that kid meant trouble."

"It's not his fault."

"You and Rosella never fight! You get along like two peas in a pod. Then Raymond Mooney comes back to town and—"

"Dave, you're not letting me talk."

"You're right." He ducked his head. "Sorry. I don't like to see you sad."

"I'm not," I lied. "I just wish it hadn't happened. I didn't want to trade Rosella for Raymond."

"What's the hitch? She doesn't like him?" Dave finished his wine.

"She doesn't want to share me. Raymond says it's natural for her to feel jealous, but—"

"Raymond says! That's big of him!" Dave snorted. Iffy materialized and refilled his glass. "I've got no use for that kid. Or his family. Look at his daddy, sitting around collecting disability. He's not so disabled he can't hotfoot it down to the Inferno every afternoon."

"I hate people who sit around in bars, don't you?" Joe Pagnani drawled.

Dave raised his voice. "You know what I'm saying! And that kid of his is nothing but trouble."

"He's a nice kid," Tommy Loors said. "He sure helped out the basketball team."

"I don't give a rat's ass about the basketball team! Do you mind if me and Liv have a private conversation?"

"No such thing in Kumquat," Tommy said, and Joe and Iffy laughed.

Dave ignored them. "The thing is this," he said.

"Real friends want you to be happy. They don't make you choose between them and someone else."

"But that's what everybody's doing, including you," I said. "I know the Mooneys, they're real nice people."

"Mrs. Mooney is a saint," Dave said.

"If you knew Mr. Mooney—"

"I've known him for years, way before you were born."

"You don't know everything about him. Don't you trust my judgement, Dave?"

"I do." He looked directly at me. "But I don't trust the Mooneys, father or son. Maybe I'm being silly. You're a big girl now and look out for yourself. Your grandmother asked me to keep an eye on you. I told her she didn't need to ask; I cared like you were my own granddaughter.

"Now, listen; I'm not going to say much more. If you have a problem, come to me. Maybe I won't be able to fix it, but I'm always here. Remember that. I know you can't talk to your mother sometimes. Seems like she's never been as strong as you, Liv."

"Seems that way." I finished my soda. "I have to deliver the papers, Dave."

He drained his glass. "I'll help you."

We climbed in his truck, Jimmy Dean in back, and drove to the *Messenger* office. The sky was a smoky lavender bowl floating one luminous cloud.

"Look at those birds on the wires," Dave said. "They look like the notes of a song."

He parked beneath the telephone pole. The blackbirds dove off, joyously noisy, a cloud of them swooping and soaring like music.

17

Mother, this is one of those nights when I need to talk to someone, and the someone is you.

The wind is howling, the chimes are crashing, the rain is beating on the windows, on the roof.

It's dark tonight. No moon, no stars. This winter goes on forever. Dave says even the ducks are trying to get in out of the rain.

You should see the forsythia. It glows like a torch, even on the grayest days. Grandmother planted it, remember? I miss her so fiercely, and the missing never goes away. No matter how many years go by, her absence feels wrong, like a mistake.

So does yours. I know you're out there, and I know you'll return. I feel you coming, like spring. We'll meet again; it's in the blood. We're mother and daughter and nothing can change that. Not even you.

If you're afraid to come home because you think I'll be mad—you're right. I'm furious, Mother. You shouldn't have run away; that's something children do. Maybe you were going too fast to stop.

I'd seen that look in your eye. I knew you were feeling frantic. My father would've held you and stroked your hair. Grandmother would've made you feel safe. But I didn't know how to help you, Mother. I didn't know what to say.

We could have worked it out. We would have been all right. Instead, you're floating around like a balloon and I'm a practicing nut; pretending you're in the shower, portraying you on the phone, hiding the truth from everyone, except for Rosella and Raymond.

Why did this sad thing happen with Rosella? She's my best friend; I couldn't have survived all this time without her. Loving Raymond doesn't mean I love her less, but she doesn't understand that, and he's just as bad. Raymond's like a bucket with a hole in it: everything I pour in runs right out. He's empty. He wants more.

Mother, how do you tell if someone really loves you? How can you be sure? I think I love Raymond, but there are all kinds of love. He's never said he loves me but I think he will. How will I know what he means?

When I was young I believed that when I thought of someone, it was because they were thinking of me; that our minds were connecting across space and time.

There was no way to test this. If I asked Grandmother to keep track of when she thought of me, so we could match our minds, I was inclining her to remember me all the time, so it wasn't natural anymore. And how could I know if this system worked in Heaven? When I thought of my father, had he thought of me first? Did Heaven—and my father—exist?

My theory doesn't make sense but I like to think it's true, and that you're thinking of me tonight, Mother, as I think of you.

Please don't imagine that I sit around mad with steam pouring out of my ears. I don't. I like being alive and I've learned a lot. I've learned how much I didn't know.

There are so many responsibilities involved in running a house—and my life. Like making myself go to the dentist. Like reading recipes all the way through before I begin. Like doing my homework and getting the phone fixed. I reported the phone to the business office.

The woman said, "Must not be too bad or you couldn't tell me about it. Will you be home between eight and five in October?"

I said, "Please be more specific."

She said, "Late October."

I said, "Monday afternoon."

The guy came out and fixed it.

Now the valves are open and the rain is soaring. The fireplace glows and the room is cozy as I sit here, diddling with my homework. Rosella didn't come by tonight. I didn't think she would but I was hoping.

The firelight shines on the spiderweb, polishing the strands silver. Inside her, the spider spins an endless filament. She rides the air. She never fails herself, she never falls.

The world is so big. How can I ever find you, Mother? Mrs. Riley says she lost her husband and I picture little old Mr. Riley, padding along an eternal hallway, peering back over his shoulder, wondering where Mrs. Riley went.

He's dead, not lost. But he's lost to her.

How could I lose you, Mother? How could I have been so careless?

Sometimes I pretend you're still here, in another part of the house; upstairs, or in your reading room. I leave the light on in there some nights.

This is one of those nights, Mother. The house shifts and sighs. My mind is restless as the wind, refusing to focus on this overdue book report before me. *What did you get out of this story? What was the author trying to say?*

I should have reported you missing right away. But I was afraid we would get in trouble; afraid you'd go to jail for abandoning your child, and I'd go to Uncle Sargent's, which was worse.

Besides, I couldn't believe you were really gone. I kept thinking you would be back any minute, any day, any week. Any month. Any year.

18

I stayed after school to watch Raymond rehearse. It was thrilling to sit in the dark auditorium and see him fill the stage. He wasn't just acting; he *became* someone else. Miss Maxwell is right; the play will be a smash.

As we strolled home his cheeks glowed pink. He looks so different at different times. I never can get a fix on his face; it's always changing, always handsome.

We held hands. His touch is still a pleasant shock. His hands are smooth and warm and dry. Years ago, in folk dancing, I was Bunky Block's partner. His hands felt like two big clams.

As we passed the laundromat Raymond declared, "I have got to get out of this town."

"Why?"

"Because it's lower than a dog's belly." He looked at me and laughed.

"That sounds like something Bunky would say."

"It is. That's what worries me." He squeezed my fingers.

"Kumquat's not so bad," I said.

"Compared to what? You haven't been anywhere."

"I went to the circus in Sacramento."

"I'm serious, Liv. Right after graduation, I'm gone."

My heart sank. "To the Pasadena Playhouse?"

"I don't know. I'm thinking about going to New York; taking a chomp out of the Big Apple. Get into some off-Broadway shows . . . I think I could support myself by modeling. Do you?"

"Do I what?" My mind had wandered, thinking how empty the town would be when Raymond had flown away.

He flashed me a profile. "Could I make money modeling?"

"Sure."

He stopped walking and took my other hand. We were standing in front of the barber shop. Tommy Loors was in the chair, all lathered up, grinning at me through the window.

"Liv, if I ask you a question, will you give me an honest answer?"

"I'll try." My stomach tensed. Was he going to ask if I loved him and say that he loved me, too? Please, Lord, don't let him drop to his knees in front of the barber shop.

"I mean it," he pleaded. "It's very important. You've got to tell me the truth. Do you think I'm good-looking?"

Surprise, surprise. His green eyes fastened on me, waiting.

"Of course I do."

"In what way?" he said.

"In every way, I guess."

"Could you be more specific? I really need to know. Do you think I'll stand a chance in New York?"

"Well, gee, Raymond, sure. Of course I do."

"How would you rate me on a scale from one to ten?"

I was on the spot. "A nine, I guess."

"Not a ten?"

"Or a ten. You're very good-looking. Everybody says so."

"Like who?"

Tommy and the barber winked at me.

"Lots of people. The girls at school."

"Who do they think is better looking than me?"

"Nobody! Can we please keep walking?" I grabbed his sleeve and pulled him down the street.

"I don't mean to sound conceited," he said. "I need an objective opinion. Sometimes I think I'm too unusual looking."

"You're not."

"What about my eyes?"

"They're very distinctive."

"Too distinctive?"

"You have beautiful eyes! Raymond, what has gotten into you?"

We sat on the bench outside the pharmacy. His warm hands covered mine.

"Look at this place," he muttered. "I'm not going to be buried alive in this town. I want to see things, do things, go exciting places!"

"You will! You'll be a big success."

Unconvinced, he shook his head. "New York is a big city."

A caravan of gravel trucks roared by, showering pebbles and dust.

"This town is so bad they're hauling it away!" he hollered above the noise.

Across the street I spied Rosella, entering the hardware store. She glanced at us, then turned away. We haven't spoken in weeks, except for unavoidable hellos. At school she looks right through me. Sometimes I pretend I don't see her.

When I think of her my heart aches. My heart actually hurts. Raymond says the pain will go away. He says this was bound to happen someday; Rosella and I were unnaturally close.

If I can't be close to Rosella, I don't want to know she exists. I want her erased from my memory. I don't want to know what I'm missing.

"Your hair looks good like that," Raymond said. He likes it long and loose. "When your bangs grow out, you'll look really great."

"In the meantime I can't see where I'm going."

"You're not missing much," he said. "Liv, I want you to come to New York with me! We could have a fantastic time."

I laughed. I'd be no more at home on the streets of New York than Jimmy Dean would be.

"I mean it! Why not? You could go to school there."

"I was thinking of the J.C. in Cedar."

It was Raymond's turn to laugh. "What a waste of time. Drive for an hour, and when you get there, you're nowhere."

"It's more like forty-five minutes," I said.

"Aren't you sick of this town? Nothing's keeping you here."

"I can't just leave."

"Why not?"

"For one thing, who would take care of the house?"

"Sell the house," Raymond said.

I was shocked. "I can't sell it! That's my family's house!"

His face softened. "Liv, I hate to say it, but your family's dead."

"Mother's not dead!"

"Maybe not, but she's gone."

The pity on his face made me furious.

"I know what you think but you're wrong!" I said. "Mother's coming back someday! I'm not selling the house and I'm not moving away! Mother would never find me in New York."

"Maybe she's not looking for you, Liv. Hasn't that occurred to you?"

"Raymond, I don't want to talk about this." I pulled away from him and stood.

He put his hand on my arm. "I didn't mean to upset you. I just don't want to see you hurt."

Dave and Jimmy parked down the street and started walking toward us. Raymond's nose wrinkled. He kissed the top of my head.

"Got to run," he said. "I promised Mom I'd take her to the laundromat."

He declined my help and left abruptly. Raymond thinks Dave is a crazy old man and Jimmy Dean is living proof.

Dave's heavy ranch boots scraped the sidewalk. "Didn't mean to scare off your boyfriend," he said.

"He has to go."

"I'll drink to that. How about a cup of coffee?"

We went into the Cough Up. "Hup!" Dave said as Betty brought our coffee. Sometimes he says hup instead of hi. The doughnut holes were warm and fragrant. Betty opened the door and tossed a cheese pocket to Jimmy.

Betty said, "See the thing in the paper about that

duck in Detroit with no head? Aside from that, he's perfectly healthy."

"You can't believe everything you read," Dave said.

"Not if it's in the *Messenger*." Betty winked at me. "This was in the national news."

"I don't care where you saw it. You can't be alive without a head. Unless you're the mayor," Dave added chuckling.

"Oh, I've got to go on a diet," Betty moaned, brushing cruller crumbs off her lips. "I've got a spare tire that won't quit. Liv, can you do this?" She grabbed a roll of flesh at her waist. "No, of course you can't, a skinny little thing like you. Doesn't your mother ever feed you? How tall are you, anyway?"

"Five six."

"Hmm," she said. "Girls aren't supposed to get too tall, you know."

"Maybe I can get those Detroit doctors to cut off my head."

"They didn't cut off the duck's head, Liv! It didn't have a head to begin with! Hey, did you notice in last week's *Messenger*? Candy Lewis and Buck Brown are engaged again."

Looking out the window I saw Rosella leave the hardware store. Through the break in the traffic she spotted me, too. Our eyes met and held—then she shifted her large package so it covered her face and walked down the sidewalk as if what she carried required all her strength.

19

Saturday afternoon was sweet as spring. The quince popped into bloom, narcissus scented the breeze, and the sky was as cloudless as a baby's eyes.

I put on my cutoffs and washed and waxed the Plymouth. Aside from a few small dents and the paint so faint it's every color, the car looked showroom new.

Heading downtown for gas, I drove past Mr. Mooney. He was going into Danny's Inferno. One window was broken and the sidewalk glittered with glass. Mr. Mooney had seen better days, too. He looked like he'd been hammered down into his shoes. He looked like he'd come through that window.

I happened to drive by Rosella's. It seemed so odd not to stop the car. At the market yesterday, I'd run into her mother. She said, "We've missed you, Liv." Her eyes were sad.

I wanted to crawl inside her coat pocket. "Me too," I mumbled, pretending to hunt for something at the bottom of my purse.

I parked in front of Raymond's house. Sophronia answered the door, her eyes glassy. On Saturdays she starts watching TV when the first cartoons come on, switches to *Creature Features* at noon, followed by *Hee Haw* reruns until five, when she breaks for an hour to shampoo her hair.

"Come on in." She collapsed on the couch, which was piled high with dingy velvet pillows. The curtains were drawn and the house was dark and smelled of canned spaghetti sauce and cats.

"Want a marshmallow?" She offered me a half-empty bag, her eyes on the TV set.

"No thanks."

She tore each jumbo marshmallow in half, catching the white string on the tip of her tongue, then slowly sucking each half into her mouth, deliberate as a lizard.

"Sophronia, is Raymond here?"

"Oh, you stupid idiot!" she said, disgusted with the actress in the *Creature Feature* film. "She goes back into the house after somebody tries to kill her! Raymond! You stupid idiot!"

He stormed out of his bedroom. "Quit yelling at me, you moron!" Then he noticed me and winced.

"I wasn't talking to you!" she retorted indignantly. "I was talking to the idiot on the TV set."

"Shut up."

"Try and make me."

Mrs. Mooney lumbered into the room with a basket of laundry.

"Don't start, you two," she said. "Hello, Olivia.

Brothers and sisters, they fight like cats and dogs."

"She's both," Raymond said.

"Drop dead, you jerk."

"I'd love to continue this stimulating conversation—"

"Big words!" Sophronia jeered. "You might fool your friends but you don't fool me!"

He moved toward her. "Raymond, don't," his mother said.

"Let's get out of here." His jaw locked tight. He slammed the front door so hard a flowerpot fell off the porch and smashed.

"Raymond, I don't mind driving."

"What's the matter, don't you trust me?" He held out his hand for the key.

"Sure . . . it's just that you're upset."

"Oh, really? How would you like that android for your sister?"

I'd always wanted a sister, but. . . . We blasted off, burning rubber. Raymond drove through town at fifty miles per hour, his face grim, not saying a word.

Careering off the highway we bounced onto the dirt road that leads to Man Eater Lake. I recalled the day when Raymond had stepped into my life again—and Rosella began her journey into the past.

He stopped the car and sighed. I looked at the lake and waited.

"Sorry to act like such a fool," he said.

"You can't help it."

"What?"

"I'm kidding! You shouldn't let her get under your skin."

"If only the Mafia would take out a contract on my sister."

"Raymond, don't even joke about something like that!"

''You're right; I'll do the job myself. Know how? I'll unplug the TV. Can't you see her, twisting and drooling. 'Just five more minutes of *Star Trek*!' she'll beg. What a pathetic picture.''

We laughed. I looked down at my hand in Raymond's hand, resting on Raymond's blue-jeaned thigh. The sun made a shining mirror of the lake. His arm slid around my shoulder.

''It's so beautiful you'd never know it was dangerous,'' I said, leaning forward for a better view.

''Am I making you nervous?''

''A little,'' I admitted. I couldn't help telling him the truth.

''You don't have to be nervous with me. We go back a long, long way.'' He stroked the vein at the top of my wrist. ''Do you know that I love you, Livvy?''

''You do?'' His green eyes had become almost gray. ''Me too. I mean, I love you, Raymond.''

''I know,'' he said, gently kissing me.

I had been kissed before; gotten goodnight pecks at the front door after school dances; fended off lips like drenched sponges. Raymond's kiss was different. The softness shocked me, electrifying my body, my mind. Every cell of me breathed his name.

''Close your eyes,'' he whispered, kissing each lid. His breath warmed my throat.

''Raymond, wait.''

''What's wrong?''

''Nothing. I was leaning against my hair.'' I lifted it from behind my back and let it fall down the front of my sweater.

He watched me with a tiny smile. ''I'm making you nervous again,'' he said.

''I want to be close to you, Raymond, I do, but I'm used to having room around me.''

"What's that mean?"

"I mean it's hard to be close to someone when you've gotten in the habit of hiding."

He nodded as though he understood. "You're honest, aren't you, Livvy."

"I used to be, before Mother left."

"You're the most honest person I know."

He tenderly kissed my fingertips then pressed his lips into the palm of my hand. My eyes filled with tears. I tried to turn away but Raymond wouldn't let me.

"You don't have to hide from me," he said, touching my cheek, smoothing back my bangs. "I want to take care of you and make you happy. Aren't you tired of living alone in that big old dream factory?"

"Raymond, please don't talk about selling the house again."

"She's been gone almost three years!"

"Two and a half."

"Do you want to rot in this town, Livvy? Do you want to turn into a crackpot? That's what will happen if you keep living alone! You'll be one of those old ladies you read about in the paper, holed up in a house full of empty cat food cans—"

"I don't have a cat."

"You're missing the point!"

"And you're making me mad, Raymond! I said I didn't want to talk about it!"

"You have to talk about it!" he said. "You have to face reality! You're covering for someone who doesn't exist! Your mother's not coming back!"

I was out of the car, walking fast up the path that led to the highway. He came after me.

"You can't run away from it, Liv."

"I'm not running; I'm walking," I said.

"I love you! I'm trying to be your friend!"

"Well, don't!"

"Listen!" He grabbed my shoulders. "Do you want me to sit around and pretend with you? That won't bring her back!"

"Let go of me."

"No, I won't! Can't you see what's happening, Liv? I'm trying to be close but you're running away! You're hiding! Please don't leave me! I've lost so much! I can't stand to lose you, too!"

His anguished words cracked open my mind. My stiff body went limp. Years of dammed-up tears deluged me. I cried so hard I consumed myself. Raymond took me onto his lap and held me, in a patch of sunlight, in the heart of the woods.

"It's all right, all right," he whispered. He patted my shoulder and stroked my hair, and I remembered my father holding Mother; and I remembered Mother braiding my hair; and my father, riding down the slide behind me so I wouldn't be afraid; and Grandmother rocking me and singing a song about sleepy pigeons coming home to roost...

Why did they all leave me? How could I ever leave their house?

"It's all right, all right," Raymond murmured. And after a while, it was true. I sat up, feeling damp and ridiculous, and dried my face on the tail of my shirt.

"I must look really great," I said.

He smiled. "You look just fine."

"I don't know why I'm acting like this."

He put his finger to my lips. "Love means never having to say you're soggy."

I laughed. At least I wasn't wearing makeup, which would have been a mess. Raymond has been after me to try shadow and mascara. It would bring out my eyes, he says.

The sun dropped behind the mountains and the air instantly cooled. He stood and pulled me to my feet. We walked back to the Plymouth, holding hands.

"I'm sorry I was rude," I said.

"You didn't mean to be."

"I'm glad you care about me, Raymond."

"I know."

He took me in his arms and kissed me. The length of his body pressed against mine. We stood like that for a long, long time.

"Let's go back to your house," he whispered, kissing my eyes, my hair.

We peeled apart and got in the car. Raymond drove with his arm around me.

He said, "This might sound strange, but will you do me a favor?"

I was not prepared to give him an unqualified yes. He laughed at the expression on my face.

"Not that," he said. "I want you to call me Roman instead of Raymond."

"Pardon?"

"I'm changing my name. Raymond Mooney is strictly hicksville. So I'm thinking of Roman Moon. At first I was going to go with Ramon, but I like Roman better, don't you?"

I was speechless. "Well, Raymond . . ."

"Roman."

"Roman . . . Isn't that kind of drastic?"

"Not really. I want it to appear on the program for the play. I was going to change it anyway. You'll get used to it."

"Yes, but—"

"What?" He looked annoyed.

"It sounds kind of—phony."

"Phonier than Rock Hudson? Rip Torn? Donald Douglas?"

"This is Kumquat, not Hollywood. The kids will tease you."

"That's their problem, not mine," he said firmly. "Do you like the name Raymond?"

"Not particularly," I admitted.

"How about Mooney? How's that grab you? It sounds like some hillbilly name. 'Raymond! Raymond Moooooney! Get out of that pig sty this minute, boy!'"

I tried not to laugh. "It's not that bad."

"Bad enough," he said.

"It will be hard to call you something else."

"That's why you have to start right now."

The subject was closed as far as Raymond—Roman—was concerned. I could imagine what Bunky Block would say. I could picture the rise of Rosella's eyebrow and the smirk in the corner of Dave's mouth.

It was Raymond's—Roman's—name to do with as he pleased. I was proud that he didn't care if he got teased. You can't live your life by what other people think. In the long run, you live with yourself.

He pulled into my driveway. "Look at this place. Vincent Price could come running out the door."

"It doesn't look scary," I protested, "just big."

He said, "This is the castle where the sleeping princess lies, surrounded by a wall of thorns. But, hark! The handsome prince arrives to wake her with a kiss."

I said, "Raymond, are you trying to tell me the hedge needs trimming?"

"I'm trying to tell you that you better call me Roman," he said, opening the kitchen door and steering me inside.

20

Everything is falling on my head. My life has become completely foreign. Even the face in the mirror is strange; the cheeks perpetually pink, the eyes peering at me from a thicket of mascara.

I feel as though I'm in the backseat of my life with no control over the driver. Where am I headed? How did this happen? Who's driving?

My math teacher, Mr. Randolph, expected Mother after school today, so we would discuss the sharp decline in the quality of my work.

"Just because it's the end of senior year is no reason to go off the deep end, Liv," he cautioned as we watched the clock's plain face. Needless to say, Mother didn't make it.

He was appalled that she had ignored his crisp invitation. He said, "It's a wonder you do as well as you do, when you get so little encouragement at home."

"I told you she had to work," I said stiffly. Only I am permitted to criticize Mother.

I couldn't tell Mr. Randolph that my work is declining because Raymond is at my house every night, cuddling with me on the sofa. He promises we'll study, then he spends the whole evening trying to talk me into the bedroom.

I won't go. The line I've drawn grows increasingly fine. He's a difficult person to say no to. About anything. As long as I agree with him, he's Mr. Sweetness and Light. If I don't agree, he's sulky and sullen. I never knew he was so moody.

I've tried to explain my feelings to Raymond. He doesn't understand.

"You say you love me."

"I do," I tell him.

"So what's the problem?" he wants to know.

Grandmother told me about sex when I was ten years old. She said, "I don't know how much longer I'll be around, and I can't count on her (meaning Mother) to fill you in."

As we pruned the roses she explained the whole business, and asked if I had any questions. Just one: Was it true, like Merry's big sister said, that a French kiss could make you pregnant?

Grandmother grimaced. "Weren't you listening?"

"Yes, but Charlene says—"

"Charlene's full of nonsense."

Grandmother rehashed the physical facts, then told me how important it was to wait until I was ready.

"When will that be?" I asked.

"It depends." She stripped off her garden gloves.

"Depends on what?" I wanted specifics.

"On you and him. You're a sensible girl. You'll know when you're ready. You'll know when you're not."

Grandmother had such faith in me. She never suspected I'd grow up to be a blockhead.

I'm not ready. What's the rush? Everything is going too fast. Raymond says, "What's the matter, Liv? Aren't I good enough for you?" Half the time, he's showing off; the other half, he's wondering if there's anything about him worth loving.

People say how lucky I am. They say we make a lovely couple. Sometimes I feel more lonely with Raymond than I ever did alone. He doesn't really listen; he watches my lips. As soon as they stop moving, he starts talking: about Hollywood, New York, how much he hates his sister, how much he hates Kumquat, how fabulous he'll be in the school play.

He's not to blame for the confusion in my life. I love him, I love his touch. But I need to open my heart and really *talk* to someone. Why can't that someone be Raymond?

Roman. We all call him Roman at school. In my mind he's still Raymond. He'd kill me if he knew that. The day he leaves Kumquat he'll forget that it exists. His old life will fall away like soiled clothes. He'll step out of it and never look back.

He wants me to go with him. He wants me to sell the house. If I sell the house we'll have lots of money; enough for Hollywood, New York and even London. We could see the world. We could buy the moon! Then Raymond will become a superstar and earn his first million. It's a shining vision.

So why won't I see how perfect it could be? Raymond gets very angry. *Don't you love me, Liv? Don't you want to be happy?*

I need to talk to Grandmother now. When she died I got so sad and scared I couldn't catch my breath. The only way to survive her death was if she was there beside me.

That was the catch.

I need someone—besides Raymond—to tell me what to do.

I need to talk to Rosella.

We bumped into each other in the girls' bathroom today. I was updating my mascara. She carefully washed and dried her hands. I stiffened, expecting the worst.

"Your makeup looks nice," she said.

"Thanks. I don't have the hang of it yet."

"It takes awhile. I should wear some, too."

"No, you look fine," I said. "I need all the help I can get."

We spoke as if we were mannequins; our faces smooth, expressions fixed, frozen in our casual pose.

"How are you?" I said.

"Fine, and you?"

"Just fine."

"That's good." Rosella zipped her purse. "See you in English."

"Okay."

I stared into the mirror. My bangs streamed back in wings on either side of my face. Someone's face.

Rosella and I have become like winter sun, unable to warm each other, distant and cool. I want to cut out the place in my heart where Rosella's name still burns.

She helped to keep Mother real and alive, long after Mother was a dream. We'd speak of her as a living, breathing person who was part of my life, not locked in the past.

Raymond speaks of Mother only in the past tense. He

wants me to think of her that way, too; gone from my life, truly dead, perhaps.

But how can that be, when I hold this postcard of the Golden Gate Bridge, mailed one week ago?

> *Dearest Liv,*
> *Please don't hate me. I'll see you soon. True blues!*
> *Forgive me. I love you. I'm on my way. I really mean it!*
> *You Know-Who*

I can't tell Rosella about the postcard; we don't talk about things that matter anymore. And Raymond would say, "For God's sake, Liv! She always breaks her promise. Don't let her hurt you again!" Each word a sharp stone thrown at Mother. I won't let Raymond kill her. I'll face whatever must be faced, and when the time comes, I'll bury her myself.

If she does come back, will I have the strength to love her, or will it drain away in bitterness and regret? I love you, Mother, but I hate you, too. Poisoned love can die a horrible death.

21

Raymond breezed in the door and kissed me. The kitchen was fragrant with the cookies I'd just baked and the vanilla I'd dabbed on my throat and wrists.

"You smell like my mother." He wrinkled his nose.

"I like vanilla."

"Me too. In cookies." He quickly ate several. Then he popped a kumquat from the bowl into his mouth, took a bite and spit it into the sink. "God, that's awful. What is it?"

"A kumquat."

"That figures," he snickered. "The official town fruit . . . I tried to call you awhile ago."

"I was delivering the paper. You said you were going to help."

"That's why I called; I had to rehearse. You're coming to opening night, aren't you, Liv?"

"Of course I am."

"You don't seem too thrilled."

"Look. I'm ecstatic!" I jumped up and down. Raymond grabbed me and nibbled my neck until I broke away from him, giggling.

"Do you care if I put on the TV?" he asked, turning it on. He likes the noise. The silence of this house gets on his nerves. "That spiderweb has got to go. This place looks like the House of Usher."

"It does not." I sat beside him on the couch.

"Do you have any coffee?"

"I can make some."

"Okay."

I went into the kitchen and filled the kettle. After a moment Raymond joined me.

"The reception just went out," he complained.

"That always happens when it rains."

"You should fix the antenna. I hate the rain." He stared gloomily out the window. "How much land do you have out back?"

I measured the coffee. "Five acres."

He whistled. "That's a lot of lawn to mow. How many rooms in the house?"

"I don't know."

He laughed. "You don't know?"

"I'd have to count."

"Let's count." He took my hand.

"Raymond—"

"Roman."

"I'm making coffee!"

"Make it later."

"We're supposed to study," I said.

"We will."

"You promise?"

He crossed his heart. We were on our way down the hall.

"Kitchen, pantry, your room, parlor." He ticked off the rooms. "What's this?"

"Mother slept in here sometimes."

He opened the next door down the hall.

"That's a closet."

"It's bigger than my room," he said.

It was stuffed with a lifetime of my family's coats and smelled of cedar, mothballs and wool.

"What's this?"

"Mother's reading room." I turned on her lamp.

"Why are all those books stacked around that chair? It looks like a wall."

"It is," I said.

His heels clicked briskly down the hall. We opened the door to the stairs leading to the second floor.

It was cold up there and the air felt damp. I left on the lights as we went. A vision of the electric bill flashed through my mind, but this was a special occasion. One night wouldn't hurt.

It was strange, seeing the house through Raymond's eyes. The furniture was lightly furred with dust. The rooms looked spacious and elegant.

"This is my parents' room."

"It's beautiful." He whistled softly, clearly impressed. "These antiques must be worth a fortune." He fingered the canopy over their bed and picked up the silver-framed photograph of my father on Mother's bureau.

"He was a handsome guy," Raymond said.

"That was taken just before he died," I said. "He never gets any older."

He nodded thoughtfully. "I know what you mean. When I'm an old man, Holly will still be twenty."

We walked down the hall to Grandmother's room. Entering, I felt like a trespasser. Raymond stood reflected in her oak vanity, touching her velvet jewelry box and her bottles of perfume. I wanted to say, "Stop. Grandmother wouldn't like you in here."

But I knew he would remind me that Grandmother is dead.

I showed him the nursery where I'd slept as a child. The bookcases, built at just the right height, were filled with books so often read their pages had turned to cloth. The rippling wallpaper, aged and faded, showed a thousand children flying skyward, clutching bouquets of balloons. On the window seat a row of well-dressed dolls watched us with unblinking eyes.

I am the person who played with those dolls. Older, yet always Olivia.

"Let's go downstairs. I'm freezing." Raymond shivered.

I wasn't ready to turn out the lights. I would come back later, after Raymond had gone.

Returning to the parlor, I stoked up the fire. He stood before it, toasting his backside.

"Fifteen rooms, counting the johns," he said. His spread legs framed orange flames.

"We have to study now, Raymond."

"Roman! Roman!"

"Roman, Roman, you promised we'd study!"

"We will! What's the rush? Will you make that coffee?"

"Mr. Randolph said—"

"He's such a duck. No wonder you're flunking his class."

"I'm *not* flunking, but if I don't catch up—"

He slid his arms around my waist. "Do you know you're very beautiful when you're frantic?"

"I'm not kidding."

"Me neither." His lips nuzzled my neck. "Just think, in a few more months we'll be free."

"Unless I'm repeating the twelfth grade." I went into the kitchen to make the coffee.

"You know what your problem is, Liv?" he called. "Your problem is you're way too serious! Really. You go around expecting the worst all the time. This isn't a rehearsal for your life, you know. It's the real thing. You ought to be living!"

Irked, I set down the coffee and cookies. "That's very inspirational, Raymond. What do you think I'm doing now?"

"Worrying, mostly. And sitting around waiting for something to happen. Like my mother; she watches TV all night, and when I ask her why, since she hates it so much, she says, 'Something good might come on.' You can't *wait* for stuff to happen! You *make* it happen!"

"I'm doing all right," I said through my teeth, wishing it were time for him to go home. I was tired of hearing what was wrong with me from someone who had so many problems of his own.

"I don't mean to get on your case," he soothed me. "I know you've been through a lot. But it's time to move on, to do something new! Do you really want to be stuck in this town next year?"

"I like it here, Raymond."

"Roman. No you don't. It's just a bad habit, a security blanket."

"Maybe, but it keeps me warm," I said.

"It's *smothering* you!" he cried, exasperated. "Can't you see what's happening, Liv? Open your eyes and take a look around! Look at this house! It's a mausoleum."

"Don't talk about the house like that."

He ranted on, disregarding the warning on my face. "It's true and you know it! Your family's gone. They're not coming back, no matter how long you wait! That's all in the past and you can't change it. All you can change is the future, and you won't. You sit here waiting for that nut to come back—"

I tried to strike him. He caught my wrist. The moment was stripped to the bone, and ugly. I hated him.

"Get out of my house." I wrenched my arm free.

"Not until you've faced the facts."

"You don't know what's true," I said.

"I know this is a bad situation. Living alone isn't good for your head."

"Since when do you care about my head, Raymond? You never listen to a word I say!"

"Roman, and you know that's not true," he said. "I love you, Liv, and I want to be with you."

"In this house?"

"No! You should sell the house. Buy something else. Go someplace. Travel. Don't you see you can do what you want! Nobody's telling you what to do!"

"Except you."

His face hardened, his eyes were flinty. "You told me you love me. That's what you said."

"That doesn't mean I'm a robot, Raymond! You only love me when I do what you want!"

"Roman," he said coldly. "That is not true."

"It is! And your name's not Roman, it's Raymond!"

He was on his feet, screaming, his face livid. "My name's whatever I want it to be! And I'm not going to be Raymond Mooney! Can you get that through your thick head?"

"Quit waving your arms near the spiderweb."

His green eyes bulged. "You care more about that stupid bug than you do about me!"

"This is ridiculous." I fought for control, summoning Grandmother's voice and cool strength.

"I agree! I don't want to fight with you, Liv."

"Then stop telling me to sell the house! It's none of your business!"

"I'm trying to help you! You don't need a big house."

"Maybe not, but I've got one."

"What's the point? You live in three rooms and the rest sit empty."

"They're not!" I cried. "They're full of—"

"*Things!* There's nothing in this house but antiques and ghosts! You need people in your life."

"Like your family for instance."

"What the hell is that supposed to mean?"

"I bet you'd like to move them in here."

"Are you kidding?" he said. "I wouldn't let them in the door."

The contempt in his voice chilled me.

"Why do you hate them so much?"

"I don't. We have nothing in common, that's all."

His face was blank, a sculpted mask. How could he share nothing with his family, his flesh and blood, his past?

"You better go," I said. "This is getting weird."

"Look, I don't want to talk about them. I want to talk about us." He moved toward me, opening his arms. Instinctively, I took a step back.

Fury deformed his handsome face. "Why are you acting like that?"

"You're acting so strange," I said.

"You're the one who's strange! Have you changed your mind? Do you love me or not? Well, do you?"

"Yes, but—"

"Yes, but *what*? Why are you screwing things up? It could be so simple! It could be so good! Instead, you want to sit here in this goddamned tomb—"

"You'll have to leave if you're going to swear."

"What are you, a nun? You've never heard people cuss?"

"Not at me, not in my house," I said.

"Look. I'm sorry." His hands were trembling. "I don't want to upset you. I love you, Liv. I love you and you don't even care! When we came back to this town I wanted to run away, but there was one good thing, and that was you. And this house—I always loved this house. It was so big and clean and nice. I used to pretend I lived here, too...I thought we could be together, Liv! I thought we could be so happy. We're all alone in the world—"

"You've got your family."

"They're not my family!" he shouted, the veins in his neck rigid. "I told them I didn't want to come back to this town—"

"Your dad didn't have any choice," I said. "The Mob would've gunned him down."

He laughed, a hideous chortling sound, like the burble of blood from a fatal wound.

"You are so naive, Livvy. You're just like a little child," he gasped.

Fear constricted my mind, my tongue. "You mean he's not an FBI guy, or a CIA agent, or whatever you said?"

"Of course not." Raymond collapsed on the couch. "My father's the town drunk."

The floor shifted. The room tilted. I couldn't bear to understand what Raymond meant.

"You lied to me?" I whispered.

"Why shouldn't I lie? It's better than the truth," he said.

My mind reeled, my brain exploded, shattering Raymond's image. I was alone in the house with a complete stranger.

"Why did you lie to me?" I panted, fighting for breath in a darkening vacuum.

"You think I want you looking down your nose at me?"

"I wouldn't—"

"You couldn't. Your dad was a drunk. But everybody else does and I'm sick of it!" Raymond spat.

"Raymond—"

"Roman."

I had to sit down. "You could have told me the truth."

He sneered, his face gaunt, all the charm starved out of him. "You're not going to sit there and call me a liar when you've lied to the whole town!"

"I didn't have any choice!" I said.

"Me neither. You don't know what goes on in my head."

"I don't know you at all," I confessed.

"Sure you do. Now we know each other better. No more secrets, no more disguises."

My mind was in ruins. I sorted through the rubble. "Did any of it happen? Was any of it true?"

"He had a good job but he got sacked," Raymond said flatly. "And he backed the car over the dog."

Hysteria clawed at my throat. I almost screamed with laughter. Almost screamed.

"What about Holly? Did she exist?"

"Of course she did! She still exists! Don't you think I can get a girlfriend? I can get any girl I want!" He waved his hands wildly. "I don't want to talk about this. Let's talk about the future. Our future."

I felt as though I had been struck with something very hard and thick. "Raymond, we don't have a future."

"Roman. Not in this town. That's why we're leaving."

"Raymond, I'm not leaving."

"Roman!" He pounded the arm of the couch. "I've told you and told you to call me Roman! Why do you keep arguing with me?"

"I'm not."

"Yes, you are! You're doing exactly what I knew you would do when you found out about my old man!"

His eyes were too large and white. They frightened me.

"This has nothing to do with your father. I trusted you and you lied!"

"Listen who's talking! You're the biggest liar around! You've lied to the whole town! You've lied to yourself! It's crazy, Liv! This make-believe crap about your mother coming back. She's bye-bye! Finito! So long and so what! If you want my opinion, you've gone a little nuts!"

"Stop shouting at me." The steely edge in my voice cut through Raymond's fury. He looked confused, and then afraid, and then he laughed.

"Listen to us, fighting like this. We don't need to fight, Livvy. We've been through so much. Life is going to be good to us now." He knelt beside me, stroking my hair. "Trust me, baby. Please don't ruin what we've got."

"Raymond, we don't have anything!"

"Roman! That's not true!" he screamed. His hands tightened on my hair. "We love each other!"

"We don't know each other!"

"Strangers don't kiss like this!"

His lips crushed mine. His teeth were sharp. He pulled me onto the floor. I struggled and fought to throw off his weight, but Raymond was on top of me.

He was making hate, not love. His fingers ripped my skin. We rolled and thrashed across the rug. When I gasped for breath his teeth sank into my neck.

"Raymond, stop!"

I kicked, I scratched, I slugged his back. I grabbed a handful of his hair and yanked.

His face was a nightmare, outraged and unknown. He looked like he wanted to kill me. But I had come too far, too hard, to die. In my face he saw that I would kill him first.

"Jesus." He stood up and straightened his clothes as if he had taken a spill. "What the hell is the matter with you? I don't have to beg for it, Liv."

"Get out." I sprang to my feet, keeping the couch between us.

"With pleasure. But let me tell you something, lady: you've got a big problem."

"Get out before I kill you, Raymond!"

"You really don't care for boys, do you, Liv? You go for your little black girlfriend."

I walked to the fireplace and picked up the poker.

"See how you're overreacting?" he said. "You're blowing this whole thing out of proportion."

"You're crazy, Raymond."

"You're the one who's crazy, living alone in this morgue! I tried to help you!"

"No, you didn't! You wanted me to sell the house so you could take the money and move to New York!"

"I wanted you to come with me!" he cried. "That's the truth!"

Maybe it was. I would never know.

"Now it's too late," he said sadly. "Too late." Picking up his jacket he casually swung it through the air, destroying the spiderweb, erasing two years.

"I loved you, Liv. I really, truly loved you."

He walked out of the house without another word.

Waves of emotion rose and overwhelmed me. I wanted to run after him and beat him until he was dead. I wanted to plunge the poker into my heart. Deep inside me a child was screaming. I began to tremble and could not stop.

Later, the phone rang. I was terrified; afraid that the sound of Raymond's voice would drive me to the place where crazy people go, and I would never find my way home again.

It rang and rang. I finally answered.

"Hello, Liv." It was the school principal. I could picture his kind face and perpetually sad eyes. His voice seemed to hold a new sorrow.

"Liv, I just had a phone call," he sighed. "From Raymond Mooney."

"Yes?" I said.

"You two having some kind of problem tonight?"

"Seems that way," I told him.

"He gave me a story . . ." The principal sighed again. "The police chief and I want to drop by tomorrow night and check things out, if that's convenient."

"Fine," I said. "I'll be here."

"Seven o'clock all right?"

"Just fine."

He almost moaned. "Well, good night."

"Good night."

For a long time I sat with the receiver in my hand. Then I walked through the house turning out all the lights.

22

I did not go to school the next day. I cleaned the entire house; dusting, polishing, vacuuming, scrubbing. Floors gleamed and windows sparkled. Vases overflowed with flowers: hyacinths, daffodils, forsythia.

I would be ready for my guests, as Grandmother had taught me.

Grandmother, how could I be such a fool? Why did I trust Raymond?

Olivia could be counted on to get the job done; she kept the car running and defrosted the fridge, balanced the checkbook and juggled the bills— Now she's lost her way, betrayed, because a lost soul said he loved her.

How will I ever trust my judgment again? I was never as strong as I'd thought. But I didn't want to be immune to love. Even Superwoman needs her Superman.

I will probably be shipped off to Uncle Self-Righteous. He'll groan and complain but will secretly smack his lips at the chance to whip my immortal soul into shape.

How can they make me leave this house?

Look at it, huge and solid and safe, an ark on a stormy sea. The tick of the clock is as steady as God, and the sun spills onto the faded rug that belonged to Grandmother's grandmother...

This is my house. They cannot make me leave.

I watered the house plants, just in case, and baked a batch of cocoa-cream clusters.

The bay window looked naked without its webbed veil. I had not seen Mama Spider. Was she hiding until it was safe to come out, or was she crushed on the bottom of one of Raymond's shoes? Again and again, my mind replayed the scene: the swing of his jacket, that awful half-smile.

This is the end. The game is over. I can't believe it's happening, yet I always knew it would. They'll make me leave this house and live with other people, and I'll be alone as I've never been alone in my life.

No. I'll be eighteen soon. I can live wherever I please. I can stay in Kumquat forever, if I choose.

Will people still like me when they find out I lied; when they realize that they've never really known me?

I need to talk to someone. I want to call Rosella. Too late; there's nothing she can do to help me. When she tried, I wouldn't listen. She was so right about Raymond and I was so wrong. I saw him as I wanted to see him. It's my own damn fault. But what is life worth if you can't believe in people? We're all we've got on this earth.

I wanted to look downtown for Dave. I ached to fall asleep against his shoulder as I had when I was a little girl. But I couldn't face his hurt when he learned I had lied to him—to him! Of all people! *Why, Livvy, why? I thought we were friends*...It was too late for explanations.

The phone rang and foolish hope flashed through my brain. It was the principal calling: Forget the whole thing. It was all a big mistake...Or it was Mother, at the market. She would be right home...should she pick up something for supper?

It was Mrs. Wallis, relentlessly pursuing an overdue book.

"You can check it out again, if you haven't finished it, but you'll have to bring it down here," she said.

"I'm sorry, I didn't—"

"I understand, Olivia. Unfortunately, I can't make an exception for you or I'd have to make an exception for everyone, and then we wouldn't have any rules."

She talked about the regulations, her duty, and the public's obligation. I was on the bridge, getting ready to jump, and she was ticketing me for loitering.

I promised to return the book and hung up. I arranged the cocoa-cream clusters on Grandmother's prettiest tray. I cooked some instant rice and ate it. Then I washed and dried the dishes and set the kettle on to boil.

I built a beautiful fire in the parlor, then walked through the house, my house, turning on all the lights. The rooms blazed. Raymond was right: The house was full of ghosts. No one could take away my memories. The past was safe in my heart.

"Grandmother, is my father really dead?"

I went to her when I wanted the truth.

"*Yes*," she said. Her eyes were red. It was the morning after the day he died.

"That means he won't come back and I won't ever see him again."

She blew her nose. "That's right, Olivia. Unless you believe in heaven."

"Do you believe in heaven?"

She stared out her bedroom window. "I don't know," she said, her voice strangled and strange. "I believe different things at different times."

"My father believed in heaven," I said. Grandmother looked surprised. "He said he'd always love me in that song."

"What song?"

"The Kumquat song. He said he'd see me again. Do people still love you when they're dead?"

Grandmother's eyes filled with tears. "You can still love them."

"But do they love you back?" I had to know.

She searched the skies and her granddaughter's eyes. Deep inside herself, she finally found the answer.

"Yes," she said.

The clock struck seven as the doorbell rang. "Come in!" I cried, flinging open the door. Startled, the principal and the police chief flinched. They were accompanied by Mayor Bobby Block, who inserts himself into every official occasion.

"Please, sit down. Would anyone care for coffee?"

Everyone would, except for the mayor; he said coffee was too hard on the old gut; he might as well drink paint thinner. I passed around the cocoa-cream clusters. The fire snapped and crackled. We talked about the weather. It was odder than a dream.

There was a knock at the door.

"That must be Raymond," the principal said. "We thought it best, Liv, under the circumstances . . ." His voice trailed off.

"Of course," I concurred. I went to the door. Raymond

stood beneath the porch light, his green eyes shining, his face in shadow.

"Come in," I said as if he were the Avon lady. He brushed past me and sat on the couch. I sat in the rocking chair.

"Well," the principal began regretfully. "I expect you know why we're here."

"I expect I do," I said, rocking.

The major jumped in. "Now, listen here, Liv—"

"I'll handle this, Bobby, if you don't mind," the principal said. "We don't want to jump to conclusions."

"All we want is the facts," added the police chief.

"I gave you the facts," Raymond said.

"We appreciate that," the principal told him, "but we want to hear Liv's side of the story."

The mayor said, "I understand you weren't at school today, Liv. That's against the law."

The principal cut him short. "Do you know what Raymond has told us?" he asked gently, gripping the brim of his hat. "He says Luna Lee doesn't live here anymore."

"She's been gone for more than two years," Raymond said.

"Let Liv talk."

They all watched me. I rocked back and forth.

"It sounds kind of crazy," the police chief admitted, "but we thought we better check it out."

"I'm not trying to get you in trouble," Raymond told me. "I know you don't believe that, but it's true."

"You wouldn't know the truth if it bit you," I said.

"Livvy, I'm trying to help you!"

"Thanks."

The principal leaned forward and touched my knee. His face was very sad. "What's the situation, Liv? Is Luna Lee gone?"

"You might as well tell us the truth," the mayor said.
The kitchen door slammed. They had me surrounded.
Then Mother walked into the room.

23

I thought I had gone insane. I thought I had invented
her out of sheer desperation. But the others in the room
looked equally stunned, particularly Raymond.

Mother gazed around the circle of open-mouthed
faces, then behind her, to see if someone strange had
come in.

"I'm sorry." She patted her long brown hair, as if she
feared it was standing on end. "I didn't mean to
interrupt your meeting."

Smoothing her skirt, she backed out of the room. I
had forgotten that she apologizes for every move she
makes, suspecting it's another mistake.

"Mother!" I leaped up and clutched her arm, before she could fade away, before she could escape.

"Livvy!" Her face was etched with wonder as she saw how I had grown and changed.

"You're not interrupting anything, Mother. You got here just in time."

"I left some groceries on the counter," she said. "Would anyone like some Fig Newtons?"

"We've been enjoying your cocoa-cream clusters," the principal told her, smiling but perplexed. The police chief looked relieved. Mayor Bobby was peeved. Raymond's face was frozen in shock.

"Mother, you won't believe why everyone's here!" I forced a giggle. "It will really make you laugh."

"Oh, good!" she said expectantly.

"They think you took off two and a half years ago and left me on my own." I gripped my sides as if they threatened to split with smothered mirth.

"Two and a half years?" she said faintly.

"That's right, two and a half years. Of course, that's against the law, and if you did that, you'd go to jail. Not that you'd ever do something like that."

"Two and a half years," Mother echoed. "That's amazing."

"I know," I agreed, "it's ridiculous, but that's what Raymond told them. Mother, you remember Raymond Mooney."

"Of course I do. How are you, Raymond?"

He stared at her as though she had arisen from the dead.

"So anyway," I said, "that's why they're here, because they wanted to make sure that you hadn't really left. Because if you had, we'd be in big trouble, Mother. Isn't that the funniest thing you've ever heard?"

Mother may be strange but she's no dummy. She knew that our lives were at stake.

She laughed; she has the prettiest little laugh. "I'm so glad you dropped by, gentlemen, so we could get this straightened out."

"I didn't think she was gone," the mayor said. "I saw her last week. Last month."

Raymond leaped to his feet with a roar of pain. "Are you going to take her word for it? Her mother's been gone! She's been living alone! She's been lying to the whole town!"

"Stop shouting, Raymond," the principal warned him.

"You think I'm going to sit here while she snows you again? She told me the truth! Luna Lee took off!"

"Lower your voice, son," the police chief ordered.

"I'm not your son! Don't tell me what to do!" Raymond's words were choked with spit. "This is so stupid! You're going to believe her, just because she's got this great big house and all we've got is a dump!"

"That has nothing to do—"

"The hell it doesn't!" Raymond thundered at the mayor. "You sit there, looking down your nose at me—"

"You're the only one doing that," I said.

He looked at me and laughed. "This is great!" he cackled. "You make me look crazy, then you tell me I'm nuts!"

"Let's calm down and discuss—" began the principal.

"There's nothing to discuss! I'm the jerk!" Raymond said. "Can't you jokers see she's getting the last laugh? Her mother's been gone! She got back this second! Unless—" A horrible thought crossed his mind. "—unless she's been here all this time and Liv was lying to me."

"I'm lost," the mayor said.

"I wasn't lying," I told Raymond.

"It was all a big lie!" He ran out of the house. I

caught up to him under the streetlight, grabbing his sleeve. He pulled away.

"You lied to me!" he cried, his eyes wild.

"Raymond, you're the one who lied! I always told you the truth!"

"I loved you!"

"You didn't!" I was crying, too. "You only loved what you thought I could do for you!"

"Don't tell me what I think!" he snarled. "You can't read my mind!"

"Why did you try to hurt me, Raymond?"

"I was the one who got hurt!" he yelped. "Why didn't you tell me she was coming back?"

"I did, but you never believed me!"

"Damn you to hell, Liv! Damn you to hell!"

In Raymond's eyes, he was the one who had been betrayed, not me.

He melted into the darkness. I went back into the house.

"Are you okay?" the principal asked. I nodded.

"Must be a lover's quarrel," the police chief told the mayor.

"Liv, where are the tea bags?" Mother called from the kitchen.

"I don't like the boy pulling my leg," the mayor pouted.

"He's been under lots of pressure," said the police chief, "with his play and basketball and all."

"We almost won that last game," admitted the mayor, savoring the memory.

"Never mind, I found them!" Mother called.

She was on her knees in front of the cupboard. She scanned my face with anxious eyes.

"What's wrong with Raymond?" she asked.

"I'll tell you later."

So many times I had longed to talk to Mother. Now there was too much to tell. There was no place to begin.

"I wonder what got into Raymond tonight," the mayor mused, reaching for the last cocoa-cream cluster.

"Full moon," the police chief observed.

The principal sighed and studied his long fingers. He knew that he didn't have the full story and that he never would.

"Seems like ages since I've seen you," the police chief said to Mother. "The last time must've been the Pancake Breakfast, and that was four months back."

"I knew I saw her last week," insisted the Mayor. "That's why I couldn't see coming here tonight."

"You called me up and said you had to come," the principal noted.

"Sure, when I couldn't talk you out of it."

"All's well that ends well," the police chief concluded. "But I think I'll have a talk with Raymond."

"Please don't," I said. "It was all a misunderstanding."

"Liv, he tried to get you in trouble."

"Looks like it didn't work," I said.

The principal stood. "We'd better be going."

"Do you have to leave so soon? Can't you stay?" Mother smiled but her eyes were fearful. What on earth would we say to each other after everyone had gone?

"Some other time, Luna Lee. Thanks for the refreshments. Sorry for the inconvenience, Liv."

"No problem," I said, avoiding his eyes.

"These kids." The mayor grunted. "You can't keep up with them. If it's not one thing, it's another."

"I'll tell you something else," the police chief said. "They're sure getting big."

"Time flies," agreed Mother.

"Good night!" I exclaimed with unintended vehemence. I waited by the fire as Mother lingered on the porch, bidding adieu to our guests. At last she returned, looking smaller than before. She nestled into the rocking chair, hiding behind her long hair.

I would not speak first. I outlasted Mother. The silence crushed her.

"Liv, what grade are you in?"

"I'm a senior, Mother. I'll graduate in June."

She was astonished. "Are you sure you're old enough?"

"Positive. I'm seventeen."

"I was seventeen when I met your father," she said, gazing into the flames.

Now I had Mother where I wanted her. I felt like rushing throughout the house, sealing the windows, locking the doors. She would not escape. She would explain what had happened. She would tell me where she had been, and why she had gone.

And I would tell her what my life had been like in all the days alone.

Finally she said: "Liv, let's never talk about this again."

"What?" I couldn't believe my ears.

"It will only make us unhappy to dwell on the past, so let's pretend it never happened, okay?"

My white-hot heart exploded inside me, drenching my mind, igniting my rage.

"It *did* happen, Mother! You've been gone for over two years!"

She winced. "I didn't mean for it to be that way."

"But that's how it was! You can't pretend it didn't happen! Pretending won't change the facts! You're not a kid—you're a grown woman! If you'd wanted to, you could've come back! Half the time I didn't even know if you were alive! Imagine what my life has been like!"

"It must've been really bad," she whispered.

"You bet it was bad! I hate being a liar! I was never a

liar till you left! But I wasn't going to let them send me to Uncle Sargent's—incidentally, you'll probably never hear from him again—and I didn't want to get you in trouble!

"So I lied, Mother! I told lie after lie! I fooled the entire town! Everybody thinks you've been here all along! They never even noticed you were gone! Frankly, I find that a bit depressing! They only care about themselves! They see your shadow and they think it's you! They say they know you, but they don't! I've been so lonely all my life, Mother!"

"I've been lonely too," she stammered.

"So lonely you never came back!" I screamed. "So lonely you never called!"

"I was afraid you would be mad at me, Livvy."

"How am I supposed to feel? You were gone for almost three years, Mother!"

"I lost track of the time," she pleaded. "I was trying to come back. I thought of you every day—"

"I thought of you, too; when I renewed your subscriptions and refilled your prescriptions and impersonated you on the phone—*can you imagine?* That made me feel so crazy, Mother! This never should have happened!"

I raged like a hurricane, out of control. "You should've stayed here! You should've been with me! I should've listened to Rosella! But I wanted to believe that Raymond really loved me. I had to! I was so lonely! What an idiot I am! What a stupid fool! I can't even see what's in front of my face! I can't even see! Look at my hair! Look at me!"

I raced into the kitchen, tore open the drawers, snatched up the scissors, then stood trembling before the hall mirror.

"What are you doing?" Mother cried.

"Cutting my bangs so I can see where I'm going!"

"Wait till you're not so upset!" she begged.

My hair fell to the floor in jagged clumps. I stared at the woman in the mirror: pop-eyed, raggy haired, loony with wrath—but nonetheless a woman. Acting like a child would not bring back my childhood. Regret would not undo the past.

Reflected in the background, Mother cowered in her chair; head bowed, draped hair shielding her face. I wanted to scream: *Stop cringing or I'll kill you!* I hated her. I loved her. How could she leave me? Why couldn't she be like other mothers? Why did she have to be herself?

"I'm sorry, Livvy, I'm sorry," she moaned. "I'm sorry, it's all my fault."

Grandmother's voice rang like a bell in my brain. *Open your eyes, Liv, and look at her,* she said. I saw a woman, not a monster, weeping by the fire, weeping as if her heart would break.

"Stop apologizing, Mother. I'm sorry I screamed. Please don't cry. Everything is going to be fine."

She lifted her head, her face pearly with tears. "You'd have to be crazy to forgive me," she said.

"You're in luck," I told her. "I'm nuts."

She smiled and shuddered with relief like a child. "You're such a good girl, Livvy; you always were. Daddy and Grandmother would be so proud."

Exhaustion flooded my veins. I had never been so tired.

"We can talk tomorrow, Mother. Let's go to bed."

"We can talk right now, if you want to," she offered.

"Tomorrow will be fine. Really. Good night."

"Good night." She hesitated by the door to her room. She said, "I want to kiss you, Livvy, but I'm afraid."

"Don't be afraid." I went to her and kissed her. I was taller than Mother. We held each other close.

"I never forgot you," she whispered. "I always loved you."

"I always knew that, Mother." It was true.

"Things don't turn out the way you plan. I wanted your life to be so *different,* Livvy! I wanted you to take ballet lessons!"

"Don't worry, Mother. You've kept me on my toes." I patted her back and smoothed her hair. "Don't worry, everything will be all right."

24

I learned lots of interesting things about Mother in the weeks that followed.

She had spent one winter at Disneyland, as a substitute Minnie Mouse, Cinderella, and her favorite character, Snow White. They had dyed her hair black, every strand the same color. "It looked like a dime store wig," she confided.

She had developed a passion for Championship Bowling. On Saturday afternoons she watched the televised games, moaning and groaning over splits and strikes.

She had been briefly engaged to a shoe repair man in Minnesota or Michigan, she wasn't sure which; she always got the M states confused. Her fiancé was nice but spectacularly unexciting. He loved to sit and smile at her. Mother got the itch to keep moving.

We never actually discussed "what happened." These tidbits of information were sprinkled into everyday conversation. I'd say, "Please pass the catsup."

She'd say, "Rex hated catsup."

"Who's Rex?"

"My shoe repair man. We were engaged. But he loves mayonnaise."

Pressing her for details was like pounding jelly. I knew less after some of our talks than I had before we began. She didn't like to be reminded of her absence. Her guilt gland, always overactive, stood by on an emergency alert.

She was determined to make up for the time we had lost, and she plunged into homemaking with a passion: cleaning, gardening, cooking improbable meals. It was odd, having someone else at the table.

"Olivia?"

"Yes, Mother." We were having our supper. The late-day sun burned on the drawn shade.

"I was reading an article the other day . . ."

"Oh?"

"About digestion. The doctor who wrote it said that it wasn't a good idea to read during meals."

"No?" I set aside my book.

"It interferes with the natural flow of digestive juices. Not to mention conversation." She smiled to show she meant no offense.

"I'm sorry. I used to read when I ate by myself."

Mother flinched. "Of course. I just thought we could talk."

"Sure." I smiled. She smiled. We waited. "Was there something you wanted to talk about, Mother?"

"Nothing special." She delicately speared a lettuce leaf. "I just thought something might come up."

Nothing did.

"Also," Mother said, "you enjoy your food more when you pay attention to what you're eating."

"It's fish," I said perceptively. "It's good."

"That is not just fish." Mother seemed offended. "That is baked scrod, your favorite."

"Baked what?"

"Scrod." Mother was becoming agitated.

"Mother, I don't even know what a scrod is."

"You're looking at one! A scrod is what's on your plate! It was always your favorite."

"I've never had it before."

"Are you sure?"

"I'm positive."

"Hmmm," Mother said. "But you like it, don't you?"

"I love it. It's great."

"When you buy fish, you have to watch out that it doesn't have a fishy smell. If it smells fishy, it's not fresh. Remember that, Olivia."

"I will."

"Oh, Livvy!" Sudden tears shimmered in her eyes. "There was so much I wanted to teach you!"

I reached across the table and took her hand. "Don't worry, I've learned a lot."

*   *   *

Several days after Mother's entrance and Raymond's exit, I was eating lunch alone at school. Rosella crossed the lawn and my heart beat hard. She sat beside me in the cool grass.

"How's it going?" she asked calmly, stretching her legs.

"Pretty good." I offered her half of my apple.

We munched busily, filling the silence. Then she said, "It's all over town that you and Raymond broke up."

"It's a little more complicated than that," I sighed. I told her how Raymond had betrayed me—and that, to save myself, I had betrayed him, too.

"You did what you had to do," she said. Her eyes were sorrowful. "How are you feeling?"

I shrugged. "I'll live . . . He's in love with Merry now."

"Poor Merry," Rosella said.

The sun warmed my skin. The trees were hazy with new leaves.

"You were right and I was wrong," I said.

"No." She shook her head. "I was jealous."

A large pink cloud sailed serenely across the sky. I said, "How could I have been so stupid?"

"You weren't," she insisted loyally. "It isn't stupid to love people."

"You can't trust them. They're scared and selfish and weak. Myself included."

Rosella thoughtfully chewed a blade of grass. "You have to take them the way they are," she said, "and not hold out for improvement."

"I guess you're right."

"I'm always right."

We looked at each other and laughed.

"It must be strange, having your mother around," Rosella said.

"That's the understatement of the century. In a way, she's the same old Mother, and in a way, she's someone I never really knew. It's different than I expected."

"You've changed," she observed.

"Mother's changed, too. She used to seem so fragile. Grandmother and I thought she was made of cotton candy and the least little lick would make her dissolve... The woman just toured the United States! She's got more bounce than Silly Putty!"

Rosella smiled. "I saw her in the market. She's pretty. She looks like she naps in her clothes."

I nodded. "She's not too handy with the iron. She presses wrinkles in, not out. But she tries so hard! She's either cooking or cleaning or baking weird cookies or giving me helpful hints— She told me if I ever get gum in my hair, I should saturate it with barbecue sauce. True blues! That's what she said!"

Rosella fell over backwards, laughing. That set me off. We couldn't stop. We arrived in class breathless. Seeing us together, Merry's friendly face beamed with relief. Raymond looked at me as though I were a stranger.

It has been several weeks since Mother returned. My life is very different and much the same. On Mondays I do the shopping and errands. Everyone tells me to tell Mother hi, and to say they'll drop by when they get the chance but they've just been so busy and time goes so fast... The pharmacist's wife reminds me to remind Mother about the weekly specials as she loads me down with paperbacks.

Mother hasn't lost her taste for romance. Her appetite for love is undiminished. She spends hours in her reading room, blissfully absorbed in other people's lives. She's tried to sell me on the books, but in my estimation, they are as far out as Mrs. Wallis's aliens.

Mother sometimes seems like an alien herself, like someone who studied this planet from Mars. She tries to fit in, but perpetually sticks out. Her observations are accurate and bizarre.

"Have you ever noticed," she began at breakfast one day, "that most cups and mugs are designed for right-handers? It's true. A lot of them only have a design on one side, so if you're right-handed you see it, but if you're left handed, you don't; it's facing away from you. So any left-handed person drinking coffee or tea with right-handed people only sees plain cups or mugs, while the right-handers see all those pretty designs. Unless the design goes all the way around. Otherwise, you've got a problem."

"You're not left-handed, are you, Mother?"

"No, but Rex was, and he always felt left out."

"I'd never thought about that," I admitted.

She laughed, embarrassed. "That's how my brain works. Not too well, my brother always said. Oh, I'm so glad you told him off! I just wish I'd done it myself."

"He thinks it was you."

"That's almost as good. I should've told off the whole family years ago! They all hate girls, even my mother. For heaven's sake, she *is* a girl! How can she hate herself? They thought girls were stupid, so I grew up with half a brain. I thought they'd finally love me, but they didn't."

"You're not stupid, Mother. You have a very unique perspective. If they don't love you, they're the fools, not you."

"Thank you, Livvy." She smiled and touched my cheek. "When you say something, I know it's true."

Mother shows me things I've never noticed, tiny wildflowers hiding in the grass. She calls me outside when the sky looks like an ocean, and she buys bars of clear green soap that grow smooth and smoky as beach glass.

On the Currier & Ives calendars in every home and store in town (gifts from the undertaker; time marches on), she showed me that the faces of the quarter moons age, from babies in January, to children in April, to faces like Grandmother's in December. I've lived with those calendars all my life and had never seen those faces.

She thinks it's normal to keep a spider for a pet. The web is being woven. Mama Spider is rebuilding.

I would not trade Mother for anyone else's mother. In her own way she did what every parent must do: she taught her child to survive. And even thrive.

Dave and I were sitting on the bench outside the Cough Up, eating doughnut holes and drinking coffee. Jimmy Dean chased a cola can up and down the sidewalk, rooting for the last few drops.

"How was the council meeting last night?" I asked.

He laughed uproariously. "Best show in town! They could charge admission. I'd pay! Hey! I saw that article in the paper about your old boyfriend. They said he should go to Hollywood. The sooner the better, as far as I'm concerned."

"I heard the play was very good," I said. "It was even reviewed in the *Clarion*. They said that Raymond was a born actor."

"That's hitting the nail on the head." Dave grunted. The mayor drove up in his pickup truck. He unrolled the window and leaned out to announce: "Dave, you heard the vote last night! Keep that pig home or he'll be confiscated!"

"You'd throw this poor little porker in the pokey?"

"In a minute! I'd throw you in there, too!"

Dave said to me, "You know what they call jail for pigs, don't you? They call it the pig pen."

"I'm serious, Dave! This is not a joking matter!"

"You'll be hearing from Jimmy's lawyers!" Dave called as the Mayor gunned his engine and roared away, oblivious to the slogan LET SLEEPING HOGS LIE emblazoned on his back bumper.

Dave enjoyed that.

Jimmy Dean snuffled up and tucked his snout into my hand, intoxicated by the sugar on my fingers. I scratched his chin. We watched the gravel trucks pass.

"How's your mother?" Dave asked.

"Just fine," I said.

"Must be funny, having her back."

"Sure is."

It took a few moments for this exchange to sink in. I was flabbergasted. "You knew?"

He nodded, chewing. "Don't worry, nobody else caught on. You did real good."

I was too ashamed to look at him. "I didn't want to lie to you, Dave."

"I know that." He offered me a doughnut hole.

"I was afraid everybody would get mad at Mother, and I didn't want to live with Uncle Sargent."

"Who could?" Dave growled. "That pill makes the mayor look like Prince Charming."

I struggled to untangle the confusion in my mind. "Why did you let me lie to you? You never let on that you knew."

"You didn't want anybody to know," Dave said. "It

seemed like you knew what you were doing." He swallowed a big slug of coffee. "When you were ready, I figured you'd tell me."

I slowly absorbed this information, marveling at his faith in me. He had known I was no longer a child. Before I knew. He had trusted me to make the right decisions.

"I would've stepped in if you'd needed me, Liv. I wouldn't have let them send you away."

I kissed his bristly cheek. He looked startled and pleased. It was the first time in years that I had touched Dave.

We finished our coffee. The traffic flowed by. There was something I had to ask.

"Dave, if I go away to school someday, will you still be here when I come back?"

"Depends how long you're gone." He chuckled. Then he saw I was serious and added, "I'll sure give it the old college try."

"You've got a birthday coming up."

"Don't remind me," he said.

"I'm making you something good."

"You don't have to give me a present," he said.

"I'm making you a *Beware of the Hog* sign."

That tickled him but he felt obliged to protest. "That's too much trouble."

"No, it's not."

"Yes, it is."

"Well, I'm going to," I insisted.

"Well, all right." Dave grinned.

25

"See how light it stays," Mother said, her face pressed to the kitchen window. "I love this time of year, don't you? Summer is coming and everything's in bloom. It makes me feel so hopeful, as if life is starting fresh, as if...I wish I could put it into words."

"I know what you mean," I said. "I feel that way myself." I stirred the pot of spaghetti sauce. "We'll be ready to eat real soon."

"Your daddy and I had some lovely summers." Mother moved to the screen door and let the breeze caress her. The flowered cotton skirt billowed and flirted around her legs. "Everybody loved him. He was such a charming man. And of all the people in the world, he married me! I never could figure out why."

"He loved you, Mother."

"Lucky me." She smiled shyly, touching her wrists to her eyes. "Why do people cry when they're happy? It must be the time of year. It makes me sappy."

"You're not sappy." I set the kitchen table.

"What will you do when school is over?" she asked.

"Work at the library this summer, then go to junior college in the fall. I haven't decided what to major in yet."

Mother found this statement amazing. "How can you decide what to do for the rest of your life? I don't even know what I want for breakfast! Is Rosella coming by tonight?"

"Yes, we're going to study." I set a pot of water for the spaghetti on the stove.

"She's such a nice girl... I always wanted a best friend."

I smiled at her. "You sound awfully wistful. It must be the book you're reading."

"Olivia, don't make fun of my books. This one is wonderful. The heroine's so dynamic!" Mother's face lit up. Her hands began to dance. "She sets her sights on something, and—blam! She goes after it and gets it! Nothing can stop her!"

"Real life is a little different," I noted.

"Different," she acknowledged. "Not better."

The can of parmesan cheese was empty.

Mother said, "I'll just run down to the store."

"That's okay, we can live without it."

"I'll only be gone a minute," she said, slipping on her sweater and picking up her purse. "Do we need anything else?"

I said, "Margarine."

"I'll be right back." Blowing me a kiss, Mother stepped out the door. I put the French bread in the oven.

I watched Mother walk into the lilac-colored dusk;

her hair loose, her step light. From behind, she looked like me. She stopped to admire the neighbor's roses, then disappeared around the corner.

The smell of warm bread filled the kitchen. The spaghetti was tender, the salad was crisp. Supper was ready. Mother still hadn't returned. She was probably at the market, involved in conversation, or busily buying everything but margarine and cheese.

She was probably on her way home.

Mother would probably step through the door any second.

Everything looked too good to wait. I decided to eat.

About the Author

CYNTHIA D. GRANT was born in Brockton, Massachusetts. She moved to California when she was twelve and graduated from Palo Alto High School. She has worked in several glamorous professions, including waitressing and file clerking.

She now lives in the country outside Cloverdale, California, with her husband, Dan, and their son, Morgan.

She wears a size 7½ shoe.